Christmas Shop Murder

Linnea West

Christmas Shop Murder

•Chapter One•

A giant roasted turkey, a big bowl of mashed potatoes, canned cranberry sauce and a pumpkin pie were all at the forefront of my thoughts. Unfortunately, Thanksgiving wasn't until tomorrow and I still had a few hours left of unpacking boxes of Christmas decorations at the new all Christmas, all the time Christmas store in downtown Shady Lake.

Well, it wasn't going to be all Christmas, all the time. But it was going to be all Christmas from Black Friday until January 2nd when it would revert back to being the Used-A-Bit store. My mother's friend Sue Peterson had opened the Used-A-Bit when I was a child and we had often gone to the second hand store to shop for new to us clothing. With five kids in the family, my parents had to bargain shop. Owning a motel didn't exactly make them millionaires.

But this year, Sue decided to change things up a little bit. Her husband Tom had passed away a few years ago and the holiday season had been hard for her every year since. This year she had decided to take the bull by the horns and get ahead of her holiday blues by boxing up all of the second hand stuff and selling exclusively holiday themed products for the month of December.

Sue was nearing retirement age, but she was

still just as vibrant and spry as ever. She was one of those people that you would have trouble guessing their age just by looking at them. Even given some context, it is difficult. She wears her hair in a short, youthful cut and the blond color appears to still be natural. I thought about the gray hairs I keep plucking out of my head and wondered if it was impolite to ask her about her hair.

When Sue had asked my family to help with her new venture, I jumped at the chance. For one thing, it helped get me off of desk duty at the bed and breakfast that my parents owned. "Desk duty" meant sitting at the desk with only a ancient desktop computer to provide any entertainment while I waited for the phone to ring. Seeing as most reservations came from online, the phone almost never rings. So I usually sit bored out of my skull with some headphones on listening to true crime podcasts on the computer. I know most people listen on their phone, but somehow my flip phone doesn't have that capability.

The other reason that I had said yes to helping out was that I love the holidays. I love anything seasonal or holiday themed. And I love them all. Not many people can get excited about an Easter TV special, but I will be there with a bowl of popcorn wearing a pair of bunny ears on a headband as it starts. Setting up a Christmas store was like a dream come true to me.

The only bad part so far was that I had eaten one too many donuts this morning. My best friend Mandy owns The Donut Hut and right now she has adorable round donuts decorated with frosting turkeys. It was a lot of sugar in one of those and I had eaten two, which I can see now was a terrible mistake, but it seemed like a good idea at the time. I just can't control myself when it comes to seasonal things.

I had even gotten to decorate a Christmas tree that sat by the entrance to the store. Sue had given me free rein over decorating it and while it had taken me a while to decide, I had gone with a red and gold theme. I had cruised around the stock room and pulled out anything red and gold that I could put on a tree. I had spent a few glorious hours hanging red and gold ornaments on the tree and wrapping it in a big red ribbon. There were some wonderful gold ornaments that looked like icicles, but they were made out of sturdy, heavy metal. Classic red and gold Christmas ball ornaments were sprinkled up and down the tree, but the best part of all had been topping it all off with a big gold star that twinkled and glowed.

Now I was back to stocking the shelves but I really couldn't complain. I was currently taking out big bubble wrapped packages and unwrapping them to get out some adorable Santa Claus knickknacks that I lined up on the shelf. I was almost done with this box and then I was going to move onto figuring out how to display a large nativity set we had for sale.

The best part about The Christmas Shop was that along with lots of mass produced but cutesy Christmas decorations, Sue was also sourcing locally made things. There was an entire table of holiday jewelry made by Jill Rooney, who lived in the upstairs apartment of the Used-A-Bit/Christmas Shop. Jill had moved to Shady Lake not long ago and while she was only able to find a part time job waiting tables, she supplemented her wages by making adorable jewelry.

I was absolutely dying over some of the things she had made to sell in the shop. There was a simple silver chain necklace with three, small wire charms hanging from it: a bell, a Santa outline, and a snowflake. Another necklace was made of red and green wires that had been bent into chains and linked together. It was thin and delicate. I had already been hinting heavily to anyone that would listen that I would love any of the jewelry being sold at the shop.

Ding ding

The bell over the door rang. It was just a regular bell, but somehow being inside a Christmas themed shop made it seem much more festive.

I looked over to see my brother Tank coming in the door. Tank is seventeen and his actual name is Tank. He is the fifth and final child and by the time

6

my mom was pregnant with him, my parents were tired of choosing names so they gave that task to us. All of us have a name starting with T, so that was the only rule we were required to follow. His name had predestined him to now be shaped like a tank, but he made a great linebacker on the high school football team. He must have come straight from school. Unlike my volunteering, Sue was going to pay Tank to work part-time in the shop.

"Hey Tank," I called out with a wave.

"Hey Tessa," Tank said. "Where can I start?"

"Sue is in the warehouse," I said, jerking my thumb towards the back. "I'd ask her because she has a whole plan for the rest of the day."

Tank nodded and as he lumbered towards the storeroom, I noticed that two more people were coming in behind him. Rich Blanchard was the owner of the new bar and grill next door, the Loony Bin. It wasn't brand new, but in a town where you only get something different every few months, it would probably be known as the "new bar" for a while. Rich was a widower who opened the bar with his adult children, but I doubted he'd be just a widower for long. He was handsome with silvery hair. Not my type but in a small town, he was quite the catch.

Jill also came in with a box in her hands that I assumed was full of more holiday jewelry. I really wanted to see what was in that box, but Sue said it wasn't fair if I set aside all of it for myself. She meekly held on to the box, shifting her weight from side to side as she looked around. Her beady eyes flicked around the room nervously. She always seemed friendly, but ready to run away at any moment.

"Hi Mr. Blanchard," I said. I had known Rich since I was a child and still fell back into my old habits. It was weird to call someone like that by their first name. "Hey there Jill."

"Hi there Tessa," he said. "You know you can just call me Rich now. It is always so nice to see you around town. We all missed you while you were away."

I smiled at Rich, but I didn't know how to answer. The time I was away was when I had been living in the Cities married to my husband Peter. But after he died in a car accident, I had been lost in life; I had forgotten how to take care of myself. I ended up back in my childhood home in Shady Lake because my parents could see I needed the help. And honestly, it has been so great to be back. The only major difference now was that my childhood home was also a bed and breakfast, but my parents always did like to keep things interesting.

"If you're looking for Sue, she's in the warehouse," I said. "Jill, she'll probably want that box back there too, so you may as well go back there as well."

Rich smiled and waved a thank you my way before heading to the back, holding the door for Jill. Once again, I was alone in the front of the store. I put the Santa I had been unwrapping onto the shelf and sat back for a moment. I breathed in the wonderful scent of peppermint and pine tree. If I could live in The Christmas Shop for the month of December, I think I would.

•Chapter Two•

The nativity set I was setting up was huge. It was meant to be a sort of advent calendar where you put one new piece out each day leading up to Christmas. That meant there were twenty-five pieces to it. It was made of solid, polished wood and would be beautiful as just a regular nativity set also. The pieces were available for purchase separately for anyone who just wanted some. I was puzzling over how to display all of the pieces without taking up too much space. Every time I got to about the twelfth piece of the thing, it started to look overwhelming on the shelf.

I stood back, puzzling about how to do it when the bell over the door rang again. I turned around and was amazed to find that I didn't recognize the woman standing in the entry. That doesn't happen often in Shady Lake. She was looking around with a sort of sneer on her face. The woman looked to be about the same age as me, which is to say an official adult who is not to middle age yet. She was wearing tight jeans with fashionable snow boots that just barely came out the bottom of a long, winter jacket. She had a hoity-toity hairstyle that made me immediately peg her as being a suburbanite. I made a mental note to see if anyone new had checked into the B&B because I would bet good money that she was probably staying there.

"Hello there," I called, waving my hand with a smile. "I'm sorry, but we aren't open yet. We open in two days, on Black Friday so you'll have to come back then."

The woman turned and looked at me with disgust like a rat had just started speaking to her.

"I certainly hope it is open for me," she said. "My name is Claire Freeman and I am the owner of this building. Are you the Sue that runs this tacky shop?"

I was pretty taken aback by the upfront rudeness. Minnesota is known for their nice which means that when we are mean, we are very passive aggressive about it and mostly smile at each other while complaining behind people's backs. It takes some getting used to, but I prefer it to people who bluntly say what they think.

"No, my name is Tessa," I started to say, but was cut off by Claire.

"If you aren't Sue, I don't care who you are," she said. "Just get Sue for me. I'm assuming she is here somewhere in this mess of holiday gladness."

I stared at her for a beat as she stood with her arms crossed, throwing off a "don't mess with me" vibe. I didn't want to mess with her, but I was also worried about how she would treat Sue. I went back to the storeroom and found Sue unpacking the jewelry with Jill at a small table while Rich was helping Tank take a few heavy boxes off of a shelf.

"Hey Sue, somebody named Claire is here to see you," I said. "She says she is the owner of the building."

"Claire?" she said. Sue stood up, puzzled. "The owner of the building is named Renee."

"Well, that is just what she told me," I said before dropping my voice to a whisper. "And between us, she was incredibly rude."

"In that case, I'll come along with you," Rich said.

Sue and Rich walked through the door into the front end while I trailed behind them, partly because I was still trying to figure out how to display that nativity scene and partly because I wanted to hear what was about to go down. I was not surprised when Jill grabbed some packets of jewelry and Tank grabbed a box and they followed me into the store. In a small town, everyone comes to look when something is happening. We just all do it in a way like we really aren't looking. By the time we got to the front, we had missed the initial greeting.

"I'm so sorry to hear that Renee passed away," Sue was saying. She looked genuinely sad. "Your mother was a good friend of mine in high school and even though she didn't live in town, we always got together to catch up when she was here."

"Yes, it is very sad, but I prefer not to dwell on it," Claire snapped. "I'm a woman of action. And I'm taking action now. I want you packed up and out of here first thing so I can get a jump start on getting this dump fixed up."

Sue looked like she was about to cry. Rich immediately stepped forward to put himself between Sue and the nasty woman. I heard Tank roughly set down the box he'd been holding and he strode past me to stand next to Sue also.

"If I were you, I'd rethink how you were talking to this nice woman," Tank growled. Tank is typically a teddy bear, but he can get himself worked up into a grizzly if you hit his buttons enough.

"He's right," Rich said, waving his finger in Claire's face. "You watch what you say. I knew Renee also and she would be ashamed by what you just said."

"Okay, maybe I went a little too far, but she would be proud of my entrepreneurial spirit," Claire said with a smirk, refusing to back down. "I've noticed this town has a lot of dogs, but is sorely lacking any place to wash and groom those dogs. So I'm turning this place into a self-service dog washing place with a few groomers. I'm sure it will make more of a profit than this place does. Not that it will be hard to do that."

I heard a noise behind me and turned to see that Jill had dropped a bunch of necklaces onto the table. Thankfully they were all made of metal so they weren't broken, but they were a jumbled up mess right now.

"You are going to make this a dog washing place?" Jill asked. "My apartment is going to smell like wet dog."

"Oh, are you the girl that lives upstairs?" Claire asked with a mysterious smile. "At least you pay your rent on time. I'll allow you to stay."

Rich started to sputter. He looked madder than a wet hen and his face was as red as a tomato. He looked about ready to explode. Sue stepped up and gently put her hand on his arm. Rich turned and look at her before taking a deep breath.

"Claire, I understand why you would like me to be out of this building," Sue said quietly. "And I will vacate, but not until January. My lease goes through December and you have no legal reason to evict me immediately. Let me get through the holiday season and then we can talk."

"I suppose that is true," Claire said. I could almost read her mind as she rolled her eyes at us. She had been hoping she could just march in and demand to shut the store down and that Sue would just give in. "I will give you until the end of this year and then I'd like you out."

With that, she turned on her heel and marched out of the door. Her foul mood had affected the room so much that the bells on the door didn't even sound cheerful anymore as they sounded for both her exit and Max Marcus's entrance. Tank and Rich decided they had to have the last say on the matter before Claire was too far out of sight.

"You just try and get Sue and her store out of here and you'll be sorry," Rich growled after her.

"How dare you," Tank said. "You better watch your back."

"Whoa whoa, what happened? What's with the threats?" Max asked, his hands full of a stack of papers he momentarily forgot about. Max worked for the sheriff's office and was currently wearing his uniform, so he must be on duty. In Shady Lake, even on duty didn't mean much if nothing was happening. Max had been my high school boyfriend and unfortunately, we lost our spouses at about the same time. So now we were back to dating. In a way, it was good because we both knew what the other was feeling. Grieving a spouse is weird and nonlinear. We had agreed not to rush into anything too soon. We were just dating for fun right now.

"It's a long story, but tell us what you are doing," I said, motioning to the papers in his hands.

He handed me one and I saw it was for the annual Christmas decorating contest. Each year, the

15

police department hosts a decorating contest and picks the top three houses to showcase. Whoever won first place was put into a statewide contest. It has become quite the competition. In fact, my own mother had tried desperately the last few years to place so that the bed and breakfast could be showcased, but she had fallen just short each year.

The houses and businesses who placed in the top three were each featured in a front page story of the local newspaper and, if you were lucky, it would also be picked up by the regional newspaper. As much as I wanted to make my mother's wish come true so that we could get the Shady Lake Bed and Breakfast featured regionally, I couldnt' stand that thought of Chelsea Goodman writing the story about it.

I had known Chelsea for years and for a reason I've never been able to quite figure out, she hates me. In return, I've grown so I can't stand her either. If she was tasked to write a story about the B&B, she would probably sabotage it in some way.

"I was just coming to see if we could hang a flyer in your window and leave some by the register," Max said, still confused. "But I can see I did not come at the right time."

I grabbed some of the flyers out of his hands and put them on the counter. Sue was still upset, but Rich nodded at me which I took as a sign that he would take care of them.

"Why don't you come with me to pick up some coffee and donuts," I said, throwing my arms into my winter jacket. "We could use a little pick me up. I'll explain what happened on the way."

•Chapter Three•

The smell of turkey was already floating through the air and the sound of kids watching the annual parade on television were exploding out of the family room. Thanksgiving morning had dawned and the entire family was here bright and early to help cook. In the state of Minnesota, a bed and breakfast owner has to live on site which means that hardly ever is it just our family in the house. But on holidays the people who are staying are usually in town for their family and so they spend most of their time out of the B&B.

I was hiding in my room for a few moments with Mandy as I told her all of the details from the confrontation with Claire. When I got back home, I looked up the guest register and Claire was indeed staying here. I figured as much because it was here or the motel and the hoity toity types tended to stay at the B&B. I hadn't actually seen her here, though, because if I had I'm sure some choice words would have come out. I'm often told I need to try to keep my mouth shut but in the moment, I forget.

"We should probably go out and see what we can do to help," Mandy said. She was always concerned about making sure she was a good guest, although she isn't really a guest. Mandy has been my

18

best friend since I was little and had spent so much time at our house that she is like the sixth child. When we graduated from high school, Mandy's parents had retired to Florida and left the Donut Hut to her so she had actually spent time with my parents when I was living out of town.

"I think you've already done enough," I said. As expected, she had brought over two dozen fresh donuts because even on a holiday, she didn't sleep in. Mandy had a deal on holidays that instead of opening up the Donut Hut, people could order donuts ahead of time and she would deliver them before getting to our house to celebrate. Unfortunately, it meant that I've eaten half a dozen donuts in two days.

"Don't blame my donuts for your inability to stop eating them," she warned. "Besides, your Thanksgiving pants are leggings so you don't have to deal with tight pants."

My love of holidays extended to my wardrobe. My Thanksgiving outfit was a pair of leggings with cartoony turkeys all over and a long tunic top that said 'Thankful' across it in beautiful writing. It was holiday themed without being too over the top, unlike most of my Christmas sweaters.

"Let's go help out," Mandy said. "We could probably get the appetizers going so we have something to eat besides the donuts."

When it comes to holiday in the Schmidt

family, the name of the game is food. No matter the holiday, we eat all day long. On Thanksgiving we start with Mandy's donuts, move on to appetizers before we eat the big meal, which is followed shortly after by dessert and eventually, leftovers dinner. It was an all day affair and at the end of the day, we always watched our first Christmas movie of the season while trying to digest the day's food.

My stomach didn't really need the reminder that we weren't even to the second round of food for the day, but I followed Mandy to the kitchen where I dutifully sliced cheese to display along with different sorts of crackers while Mandy dumped olives and pickles into bowls.

I managed to steer away from most of the appetizers so that once we were all seated at the table for real dinner, my stomach had plenty of room for all of the traditional foods. For Thanksgiving, we used the table downstairs in the dining room where we served guests their breakfast. We also set up a card table just off to the side for the kids. There were only three kids so far, but once someone else decided to have a few more we'd need to expand the kids table.

For now, the large, solid wooden table was lined down the middle with a festive maroon runner that had the outlines of gold leaves stitched on it. On top were platters with sliced ham and a big one holding the whole turkey. The meat was flanked by large bowls of mashed potatoes, scalloped corn, and stuffing. A tureen held homemade gravy and loaves of fresh baked bread were set out with butter dishes at the ready. There was even a bowl of canned cranberry sauce that had been ceremoniously dumped out of the can in one piece and set next to my sister Trina's spot. She usually ate a can of cranberry sauce all by herself.

We all floated to our spots and began my favorite Thanksgiving tradition of all. We went around the table and each of us took a turn saying what we were most thankful for. We couldn't repeat what someone else said and any genuine answer was accepted. This year, I said that I appreciated the comfort of family, friends, and my hometown.

Then my dad stood up and carved the turkey. No one was allowed to take any food until my dad had carved and distributed some turkey to everyone's plate. After that, it was a semi-controlled free for all. As we stuffed our faces with the delicious feast, the talk turned to the confrontation at the Christmas Shop. Of course Tank and I had rehashed it all for our parents, but now we took turns telling the entire table all of the nitty gritty details.

"What do you think you're going to do about it?" my dad asked as he quietly buttered his piece of bread.

"I'm sure not going to let that woman come in a

bully Sue, that's for sure," Tank said, slamming his fist on the table. We all jumped as he raged on. "She thinks she can just come in and kick out a hard working business owner to open a dog washing store? She's got another thing coming."

"And you Pumpkin? What are you going to do?" my dad asked calmly before taking a bite of bread.

I sat back and thought about it for a moment while I ate another piece of turkey. I had thought a lot about what had happened, but not so much about how to respond to it. I didn't technically work for Sue, but I enjoyed volunteering to help her.

"I think I'll volunteer to help out a bit more," I said. "If I can just help her make a good profit this holiday season, maybe Claire will rethink her plan and let Sue keep the Used-A-Bit open."

Tank snorted and I shot him a look. I remembered what it was like to be seventeen and think I knew exactly how the entire world worked. He sheepishly went back to eating his mashed potatoes.

"I think that's probably the best idea," my dad said. "If anyone else is able to volunteer their time, that would help Sue out a lot. Or maybe just spread the word about the Christmas Shop. The more we can do without Sue spending money on personnel or advertising will help. Except you Tank, obviously you are her one employee."

Everyone started murmuring around the table, planning and plotting with each other about how they could best help Sue and the Christmas Shop. One thing is for sure: when you ask the Schmidt family for help, by golly we will give all the help we can.

•Chapter Four•

Black Friday dawned much too early. I had worked retail in high school and remembered dragging myself to my car at four in the morning to go in and ring up purchases of shoppers who were much too enthusiastic much too early in the morning. I have vivid memories of standing at my register when they opened the doors, watching people come running in to grab a shopping cart with one hand and a complimentary cup of coffee with the other hand. While the coffee was a great idea, most of it ended up on the floor as the customers ran to shove deeply discounted toasters and DVD players into their cart. It had not been a great experience and I had vowed to never work Black Friday again.

But here I was again, thirty years old trudging through the frost to the old station wagon I drove while clutching two travel mugs of coffee I managed to pour myself so I could go work a cash register once again. I did want to congratulate myself on thinking of bringing two coffee mugs because as I settled myself into the car, one of them was close to being drained already and I knew I would finish it before I even got downtown to the shop

It was my own fault. I had volunteered to work the early shift so that Tank could come in later. He

24

had been so tired lately and out and about at all hours of the night. I remembered being in high school and sacrificing sleep for fun with friends, so I didn't fault him for that. But if we were truly going to help Sue, he needed to be well rested to help with the Black Friday rush. It was the grand opening of the Christmas Shop today, so we were hoping for a big crowd.

I wound the station wagon around the lake that sits in the middle of Shady Lake as it's namesake. Thankfully the streets were not slippery today but when they were, the winding road could be treacherous. As it was, it was pitch black with only the street lights to shine a little light down which I was grateful for because I was realizing the headlights on the station wagon desperately needed to be cleaned.

As I parked in the public lot across the street from the Christmas Shop, I could see Sue standing on the sidewalk outside. She was rubbing her mittened hands together and I could see her breath as it hung in the cold air. I hoped she hadn't been waiting too long because it was so cold, but I figured I could make up for it by running out for coffee and donuts a little later. It was so early that Mandy was still in the process of making the donuts for the day. That was a discouraging thought.

Even my winter jacket couldn't keep out the

cold enough. If November was already this cold, I shuddered to think what the rest of the winter would be like. I pulled my hood up onto my head after I locked my car and hustled across the street. It was so early that the traffic light wasn't even on yet. Shady Lake didn't get a lot of traffic at night, so the streetlights downtown switched to just a flashing yellow light at around midnight and switched back to using all of the colors around five.

"Hi Tessa, I'm awfully glad you agreed to help out at such an early hour," Sue said cheerfully. She was beaming from excitement. "I know there isn't much to set up right now, but I want to make extra sure everything is in place for the grand opening and I could sure use a second pair of hands."

"Well it was me or Tank and I just knew that even if he was able to get himself out of bed, he would be walking around like a zombie for a few hours before actually waking up," I said with a smile. Even yesterday Tank had been a zombie until after the appetizers had been set out. "I thought I was the better choice."

Sue laughed a twinkly sort of laugh. She was so genuinely happy that she looked about to burst. She pulled a bunch of keys out of her purse and started sorting through to find her key for the store. The keyring was so large that it looked like every key she had ever had to anything was on it. I could see keys of all shapes and sizes, from car keys to gym locker keys. After looking through them all a few times, she looked up at me with a puzzled expression.

"That's odd," she said with her eyebrows knit in confusion. Her keys jangled as she kept looking through them. "I don't have my key."

"You don't have your key?" I said. That didn't seem like a good sign for opening day, although judging by her key ring I could understand how she had misplaced it. "Where else could it be?"

"I guess it must be in the door," Sue said with a shrug. She slapped her forehead lightly. "I'm a bit more forgetful than I used to be."

I was not surprised in the least that she couldn't find her key in all of that mess, I just hoped the key would be in the door otherwise the entire Grand Opening would be totally derailed.

"I'll check the door, but why would you take the key off of the keyring?" I asked.

"Oh, I'm just so excited about the grand opening that I probably took it off so I wouldn't lose it," Sue said with a laugh. "And then look what I did. I lost it. It must be somewhere around here though."

I walked up to the front door as Sue continued to fumble with her keyring and sure enough the key was in the lock but the door was also cracked open. It wasn't open much because we hadn't even noticed it from a few steps out, but that was probably because it was still so dark. The door was open enough to make me suspicious.

"Sue, the key is here but the door is also open," I said. "I'm not sure we should go in. Maybe we should call the police to come check it out first."

"Oh, it's probably nothing," she said with a smile. Nothing was going to get her down today. "I'm sure I just didn't get it all the way shut and the wind blew it open a little."

I didn't think that sounded right as the door in front of me was one of those old, solid wood doors that was pretty heavy. But maybe she was right. Either way, we needed to get inside to get things set up for the Grand Opening. The only problem was that the light switches were all at the back of the store so we would have to walk through the darkness to get there. That did not sound like a fun way to start my morning.

•Chapter Five•

I opened my large purse and dug my arm straight down to the bottom. There was a heavy duty flashlight down there that would come in handy. Ever since Peter had died, I had found myself starting to panic if I was ever somewhere where it was too dark so I had bought a giant pack of heavy duty flashlights at a club store and planted them around everywhere I would possibly need one. It weighed down my purse quite a bit, but also came in supremely helpful at times like this.

Sue looked confused as I pulled out the big, blue, metal flashlight and hit the rubber button to turn it on. The powerful beam reflected off of the glass of the front window and lit up where we were standing. If I was going to carry around a flashlight, I wanted to be carrying one that really worked.

"I don't think we should go charging in there, just in case," I said. I tried not to let my voice shake. It wasn't the open door I was afraid of; it was the utter darkness of the store. "Let me go first so we don't get caught unaware by anything that may be in there."

"Oh Tessa, I think you are just being silly," Sue said with a giggle. "Caught unaware by what? But if it makes you feel better, then lead the way and I'll come behind."

I slowly pushed the door open and shone my flashlight around the room. It didn't look like anyone had been in here stealing anything or causing mischief. Everything looked to be in place, so I slowly started to make my way to the back of the room.

The Christmas tree next to the front door was still decorated beautifully. The table of jewelry looked like it hadn't been touched at all. The large, wooden nativity set was still in place on the shelf. From the front door, everything looked okay, so I pushed on.

As I walked, I shone my flashlight around all of the displays and aisles. All of the shelves were as neat and tidy as we had left them two days ago. A sparkle of light flashed behind me. I jumped, unsure of what had just happened. When I turned, I saw that Sue had plugged in the large Christmas tree by the door that I had decorated earlier in the week. The familiar glow was somewhat comforting, but I knew I needed to keep going. Sue gave me a sheepish shrug and I knew that I was being a bit too jumpy.

I kept slowly trudging through the store flashing my light all over. I know Sue thought I was being ridiculous, but something about that open door had given me a bad feeling, even if it was barely open at all. Until I looked at every inch of this store, I would be nervous and jumpy.

Suddenly my flashlight hit a large, shadowy object on the floor towards the back of the room. I stopped dead in my tracks, too far away to tell exactly what it was. But there was something about it that I just didn't like. The pit of my stomach felt heavy as I looked at it. I decided that I would need to take a closer look, no matter how badly I wanted to just turn and leave.

"What is it Tessa?" Sue called. She was still standing by the Christmas tree, nervously rearranging a few ornaments and straightening out the tree skirt and fake presents underneath.

"There is something big on the floor over there. It isn't moving, but I don't know what it is."

"Oh I'm sure it is probably that giant, red ribbon thing that Rich brought over to cut for the grand opening," Sue laughed. "I can't believe he spent so much time tracking down where to buy one. You should have seen him carrying it over. He looked like he'd shrunk. I laughed so hard I nearly split a seam."

But the shape on the floor did not look like a gigantic ribbon. It looked too dark to be a big, red ribbon. It was too far away for my flashlight beam to really hit it properly though. I'd have to get closer to figure out exactly what it was.

"Stay there," I said. "I'm going to make sure of what it is."

I crept slowly towards the object. I was hoping that I was just being silly and would find that it was indeed the ribbon, but I had a bad feeling about all of this. Instead of being red and shiny like the giant ribbon, the object on the ground stayed black even as my flashlight beam hit it better.

"It's just the ribbon, isn't it," called Sue from over by the door. She was still giggling at the memory of Rich carrying the gigantic ribbon down the street, but I was too focused on the object to laugh along.

As I inched closer, the object took on a distinctly human shape. I feared for a moment that it was someone sleeping who I would accidentally startle awake. Shady Lake didn't tend to have a large homeless population and those transients we did have were steered towards the shelter that is run by one of the churches in town, especially if it was wintertime. Minnesota winters can be downright brutal and we don't want anyone to be stuck outside.

I shone my flashlight towards where I thought the face should be to try and catch a quick glimpse but couldn't see anything. Whoever it was had their arm thrown over their face. I started to get a bad feeling in the pit of my stomach. If this person was sleeping, they were a very heavy sleeper.

I looked around a little bit to look for some clues as to who this might be. If it was a homeless person, they didn't appear to have much luggage with them. Wouldn't a homeless person have some bags along with them? Further down the aisle was a larger bag that might have been either a purse or tote bag, but I couldn't tell in the dark and either way it wasn't big enough to fit someone's entire life. My flashlight beam also caught a twinkle of something gold laying under the lip of one of the shelves. I filed that away in the back of my mind to look at once I'd figured out who was sprawled out in the middle of the aisle.

Gently, I put my foot on the person and shook them, just a little bit to try to wake them up. I wanted to make sure I had my hand free in case I needed to defend myself. Some people startle awake and after a few bad experiences trying to get my brothers out of bed and ending up being hit in the face, I didn't let myself be caught unaware.

The person rolled over, but didn't seem to wake. I was about to kneel down and try to shake the person again, this time with my hands, but Sue must have found her way to the back. All of the lights of the store suddenly flipped on, bathing the entire store in bright lights.

I'd been in the darkness so long that the lights hurt my eyes and I instinctively squeezed them shut. I knew I would have to open them to figure out exactly who was laying in front of me, but I wanted so badly to just leave them shut. After a moment, I told myself that this person may be having a medical emergency and need help. So I summoned up my courage and opened my eyes wide.

Once my eyes adjusted to the sudden light, I saw exactly who it was. Laying in front of me dressed all in black was Claire Freeman. She was laying in a pool of liquid and she wasn't sleeping, but she definitely had a medical emergency that we were a bit too late to help with. A giant, metal icicle ornament was sticking out of her stomach.

•Chapter Six•

The Christmas Shop was supposed to be opening up at six that morning for all of the early Black Friday shoppers. Instead, Sue and I were sitting on folding chairs at the back of the store while the police milled around. The red and blue lights were flashing in from the street, looking oddly seasonal. That may just be because I was surrounded by holiday ornaments, but I was looking for any reason to look on the bright side after finding another dead body in town. This was becoming a coincidence that I hope didn't keep repeating itself.

"Are you ladies doing alright?" Max asked. He put his hand on my shoulder for a second longer than he would for anyone else. He couldn't show any PDA while he was on duty, but I could tell he was worried about me.

"I think we are okay," I said glancing at Sue's crestfallen face. "Thank you for putting up the barriers to keep people back. I know we are both pretty upset about not only what happened, but the fact that we can't have our grand opening today like we were going to."

Max had been thoughtful enough to tape a very wide area outside the front door which was helping keep the looky-loos at bay. We were supposed to have people lined up while Sue cut a big red ribbon, not to watch a dead body be taken out from behind police ribbon.

The worst looky-loo of all was Chelsea, who kept trying to duck under the tape and come take pictures through the front window. Thankfully, there wasn't much to take pictures of as Sue and I were too far back to be seen and the body was behind a few of the shelves.

"We do have a question for you, Sue," Max said. "The key that was found in the door, whose is that?"

"It's my key," Sue said quietly. She was clutching a gray blanket around her shoulders that one of the officers had given her. It wasn't cold in the store, but the chill of death hung in the air. "I'm always forgetting where I put it. I guess when I locked up two nights ago I forgot to take the key with me."

Max wrote down everything she said in a little spiral notebook while he nodded his head to show he was listening. He was so handsome, but I couldn't think about that too much right now.

"And who all has keys to the store?"

"Not many people do. It's just me, Tank, Jill, and Rich. That way I know that if I lose my key, at least one of the other three people will have their key and probably be close by the store to help let me in."

"And you say you left your key in the lock?" Max asked.

"I'm not sure," Sue said with a shrug. "I must have because that is where I found it."

"I can tell you that the key was there when we got here," I said. I had the bad feeling that they were trying to accuse Sue of having had a hand in whatever happened and I couldn't let that happen.

"Thank you Sue," Max said. "Just hold tight here for a moment."

Max walked over to his boss and started relaying what Sue had just said. They seemed to be discussing something and I had a bad feeling that it was about whether Sue had been the one to kill Claire. I knew I had to do something, so once Max seemed to be done with his conversation, I marched over to confront him.

"I hope you don't think Sue had a hand in this," I said. "You've known Sue at least as long as I have. You know she would never do something like this."

"You know I can't discuss an open investigation with you, even if you were the one to find the body," Max said. He looked around and dropped his voice lower. "But here are the facts. Claire threatened to close Sue's shop. Claire was found dead in Sue's shop. Sue's keys were in the front door."

"But Claire was stabbed with one of those

ornaments," I said. "Even if it was incredibly sharp, do you really think little old Sue could have done that?"

Max took a deep breath and shrugged his shoulders. He seemed a bit exasperated with me, but then again he always seemed like that when I started to pry about an open investigation.

"I do have some other suspects in mind," he said. "Claire had only been in town for two days, but she certainly hadn't made herself any friends. In fact, I'd venture as far as to say she had made herself some enemies."

I thought again of Claire's entrance to the store the other day. She hadn't seemed to care what we thought of her. She had her plan and she was going to follow through with it no matter what. The way she had gone about it had angered everyone, some of us more than others.

"I'd have to agree with you there," I said.

Max looked around and saw that no one was paying much attention. He reached over and grabbed my hand. His large hands were warm and familiar.

"I need to get back to work," he said. "Don't worry, I don't think we will be holding Sue. We will let you guys go soon, I promise."

I nodded and squeezed his hand. He looked me in the eye and I melted a bit. Max's blue eyes had always been my favorite. I walked back to my chair next to Sue and put my hand on her arm as I sat back down. This poor woman had been through enough. The last thing she needed was a murder in her brand new shop. I couldn't help but feel terrible, even though the only thing I'd done was to find the body.

"Sue, why don't I go see if we can leave," I said quietly. "I know I could use some coffee. I could treat you over at the Donut Hut."

Sue sat still for a moment before giving one curt nod of her head. I flagged down a passing officer and asked if we were okay to leave. After checking with a few other officers, Sue and I were told we were free to go, but that we weren't to leave town. Apparently they had forgotten that the Christmas Shop was supposed to open that day, so it wasn't like we had a vacation planned.

We grabbed our winter jackets and headed towards the front door. I thought briefly about trying to sneak out the back, but my car was across the street so I'd have to head that way eventually anyways. The bell sounded as we left, sounding less and less jolly each time it rang today.

Max had taken the police caution tape and roped off the entire area from the front door to the street across the sidewalk. It was too cold for anyone to actually be waiting on the other side of the tape, but I could feel eyes on us from storefronts and cars as we came out.

39

"Can I get a comment for the paper?" a voice hollered out of a parked car.

I didn't even have to turn around to know that voice. Chelsea Goodman was my high school nemesis and a reporter for the local newspaper. There wasn't much to report in Shady Lake, so whenever something big happened, she was on it like a flea on a dog.

"No comments from anyone Chelsea," Max shouted from the doorway. I turned to mouth a thank you at him and he winked at me.

Sue clutched at my arm as we started towards the Donut Hut. I had sent a quick message to Mandy to tell her we were coming. Mandy had quickly sent a message back to tell me that we could come in through the kitchen to have a bit of privacy.

We ducked under the yellow tape and walked quickly, both because of the cold and the eyes that I could still feel on us. As we passed by the Loony Bin, the door slammed open and Rich came running out with Ronald Green, the mayor of Shady Lake, following close behind. Rich ran up to Sue and put his arm around her protectively.

"Sue, I heard what happened," he said, looking right into her eyes. "Are you alright?"

"Yes, a bit shaken up, but I'm alright," she said. Sue looked a lot more comfortable now with Rich holding her close to him. The way Rich was holding her was a bit more intimate than friendly.

"Tessa, are you alright?" Ronald asked. Ronald had obviously been having breakfast at the Loony Bin. The Loony Bin didn't serve breakfast, but Ronald and Rich were close friends and often had breakfast there together.

Ronald had a napkin tucked into his collar and spread over his sweater vest. His round tummy poked out over his pants, showing why people often called him Mayor Panda. Well that and because he was mild-mannered and was usually eating.

"I'm alright Ronald, thank you for asking," I said. Ronald's love for Shady Lake and all of the people who lived here was evident. When he asked if you were alright, he genuinely wanted to make sure you were alright.

"Why don't you let me take you home?" Rich said to Sue. She nodded and looked at me, wanting to make sure I was alright with it.

"Is that okay with you Tessa?" Sue asked. "I think I'd just like to go back home and rest a little bit. Rich will make sure I get there in one piece."

I couldn't say no. Sue looked so at peace with Rich by her side that I knew I had to let her, even though I didn't want to let that scared woman out of my sight. Ronald checked one more time to make sure I was alright and then went back into the Loony Bin to finish his breakfast.

41

I said my goodbyes and assured her I would call her that evening to discuss what we were going to do about opening the store. As Rich ushered her to his car, I pulled my winter coat close around me and shuffled on towards the Donut Hut.

•Chapter Seven•

I walked to the Donut Hut as fast as I could and burst in through the alley door into the warm kitchen. Mandy was standing there with a carafe of coffee and some donuts on a plate. Mandy's love language was providing warmth in the form of baked goods, coffee, and a warm place to sit. She was an ideal Minnesotan woman in that regard.

"Where did Sue go?" she asked, her face drawing up in concern as the door swung shut behind me.

"Rich popped out of the Loony Bin and offered to take her home," I said. "She decided she was pretty shaken up and wanted to just go home. So it's just me."

"Well, I can't blame her for that; get your jacket off and come sit down," Mandy said. She turned and shuffled off to arrange a place for us to sit in the kitchen.

I hung my jacket on a peg and sat down at a stool at the big work space in the middle of the kitchen. Apparently, I had caught Mandy right as she was making some cookies because the big metal table was full of ingredients and most of it was covered in flour, except the area where we would be sitting which had been thoroughly cleaned.

43

While Mandy made a great living just selling donuts, she had also expanded into offering cookies during the holiday season. She made a great kit where she provided cut-out cookies and decorating supplies for busy families to still be able to decorate together. Honestly, I've told her she could raise the price on it significantly and still make plenty of sales, but she told me she wants all sorts of families to be able to afford them.

Mandy had a hot cup of coffee poured and ready for me. I grabbed a donut that was frosted white and sprinkled with red and green sprinkles and took a big bite. I usually couldn't say no to a seasonal donut and I definitely wasn't going to start now.

Mandy waited and took small sips of her coffee as she waited for me to start the talking. We had been friends for so long that she knew to wait it out. While I may have a bad habit of blurting out whatever I'm thinking, I also occasionally like to think through things first. Mostly I was just thinking about how somehow she could sit there sipping her coffee without a donut to eat with it. I envied her self control especially because it meant she was slim and trim. Sometimes I got jealous of her ability to make delicious sweets all day without eating them all, but then I remembered that it meant there were more donuts for me to eat and that made me a little happier.

Finally, I had eaten half of the donut and drank a cup of coffee. I refilled my cup and told Mandy the entire story of the morning, from arriving at the shop to everything that the police had been doing at the shop. I ended with how cozy Rich and Sue looked together as I walked to the Donut Hut.

"Did they really think Sue could have done it?" Mandy asked.

"They were pretty suspicious about her keys being in the door," I said. "And it was a little weird that she took the key off of her keyring to close up shop but as I pointed out, I don't think she'd be strong enough to stab someone with the ornament."

"Not to mention Sue has never hurt anyone in her entire life," Mandy said. "I don't think she's ever even said a bad thing about anyone ever."

That was probably true. Sue was one of those women who would always compliment you on something when she saw you and she was the first to bring over a casserole and flowers if someone had a baby or was sick. Sue volunteered for anything and everything she could from raking lawns for elderly neighbors to standing on the corner to solicit donations for the Fourth of July fireworks. She was also the type to remember every little detail and would ask you about them. Sue always seemed to care a great deal about every citizen of Shady Lake.

"You were there when Claire confronted Sue,"

Mandy said after taking a sip of her coffee. "Who else heard about her plan?"

"It was me, Sue, Rich, Tank, and Jill," I said. "And Max walked in right at the end, but he didn't hear what happened. He just saw Claire walk out and heard both Rich and Tank threaten Claire."

Mandy grimaced and I agreed. The last thing you wanted was a police officer to hear you threaten someone who is murdered the next day. Mostly I just thought it was good because for once, I was not the one saying the wrong thing at the wrong time.

Mandy's phone let out a small jingle of a bell. She pulled it out and checked her messages. A puzzled expression pasted itself firmly on her face. I rolled my eyes at her before I could stop myself.

"Where is your phone Tessa?" she asked.

"I don't know, why?" I asked. I wondered if she remembered that I had a flip phone. If she was looking at something on social media, which she did a little too often in my opinion, then I wouldn't be able to see it until I went home and logged onto my computer.

"Because your mother just texted me," she said. She handed me her phone and I saw the message from my mother.

If Tessa is with you, please tell her to check her phone. I've been trying to get a hold of her for a long time. Thanks love.

46

I stood up and walked over to my jacket. I reached into my pocket and found my phone amongst gum wrappers and loose change. It was on silent, which was one of the downsides of the flip phone. There was a switch on the outside to put the phone on silent and somehow I managed to bump it all of the time, so I was frequently missing messages and calls. But that was not enough to convince me to go back to a smart phone, no thanks.

I flipped open the phone as I walked over to the stool and saw that my mother had in fact called me ten times and sent me five messages of increasing emotion.

Are you okay honey? Let me know soon.

I hope everything is good. Call me.

I'm starting to get worried. I need you to call me soon.

Tessa Schmidt, you are going to be the death of me. Please answer me.

Emergency. Get home now. We need you.

My mother was not one to get herself worked up into a tizzy, so I knew something was wrong. And it wasn't just that I had stumbled across a dead body that morning. Something else must have happened that my mother wasn't willing to discuss over text message. My mind started spinning over the possibilities and I knew I needed to get home as fast as I could.

"I've got to go Mandy, I think something else must have happened," I said as I showed her the messages from my mother.

Mandy nodded. She knew Teri Schmidt well enough to know that this was not typical of her. I ran for the door before Mandy shouted to me.

"Hold on Tessa, I think you need these."

I turned around and Mandy was holding a box of donuts decorated with a Christmas theme and a styrofoam cup of coffee for the road. I pulled my jacket on and smiled at her as I grabbed them. She really did know me better than anyone else in my life.

As I did a funny shuffle-run to avoid falling on any ice on my way back to my car, I wondered what in the world could be happening back at the B&B. Whatever it was, I vowed to leave the donut box shut until I figured it out. No road donuts for me.

•Chapter Eight•

As soon as I parked the station wagon at home, I could see my mother standing in the front window. She looked relieved as I waved at her. I grabbed the box of donuts off of my passenger seat and ran inside as fast as I could, taking care to avoid the ice on the front porch steps. No matter how much salt we put on it, it just kept coming back. We actually had a large sign posted on one of the columns next to the stairs to alert customers to the ice and took care to warn everyone about it. We had been lucky so far with a few slippery close calls, but nobody getting hurt.

I pushed open the front door and held out the box of donuts towards my mother. She smiled a vague sort of smile, but I could tell she was still worried. What was going on?

"Mandy insisted I bring some home," I said as my mother took the box out of my hands.

"What a sweetheart Mandy is," she said. "But I'm afraid donuts won't help us much right now. The police have come and taken Tank in for questioning."

I could feel my eyes widen. Sure he was a big teenager, but he was still just a kid. My mother was wringing her hands and her face looked pale. I wanted to give her a hug, but I didn't want to squash the donuts.

"The police let your father go along as Tank is still a minor, so that is something," she said. She sounded like she was trying to convince herself that my father going along helped the situation, but she wasn't doing a good job of it. Her voice shook as she talked.

She turned and walked quickly towards the kitchen with the box of donuts in her hand. I followed along behind without her telling me to because I needed more details. I didn't like how wrapped up this family already was in a murder.

By the time I got to the kitchen, my mother had gotten a plate out of cupboard and was cutting into a donut with a fork and knife. She hated to get her fingers dirty, so she ate everything with a fork and knife. As a kid I thought that was normal until I ate dinner at someone's house and noticed that I was the only one who asked for a fork to eat a hot dog on a bun.

I knew she must be extra stressed if she was eating a donut. A few years ago, my mother decided to try to be healthier and sweets was one thing that she had mostly cut out of her life except for special occasions. Eating a donut on a day that wasn't a holiday meant she was not feeling like herself, especially after all of the sweets we had ingested the day before.

"Okay Mom, start from the beginning. What

happened?"

"The police came up and knocked at the door. They asked if Tank was home and when I said he was, they told me to go get him. Thankfully he was in the living room with your father, so I was able to get both of them at the same time."

She stopped and took another bite of her donut. It was almost like looking into my future. I couldn't help myself. I grabbed one of the donuts and took a big bite. The sweet taste almost made me forget why I had to go home in the first place. Almost.

"So then what happened?" I prompted after waiting and chewing a while.

"The police officers were very polite and said they needed to take Tank in to question him about the murder," my mom said quietly. "They didn't outright say it, but Tessa I think he is a suspect."

As much of a surprise as this appeared to have been to my mother, a part of me had seen it coming. I had hoped the cops would go a different direction, but Max had been right there to hear both Rich and Tank threaten Claire as she left the store that day.

"I'm glad Dad could go with him," I said. "But I think you are right. Unfortunately, he made a threat towards Claire as she was leaving the store the day before Thanksgiving and he wasn't exactly quiet about it."

My mother nodded, but I could see the tears

forming in her eyes. While she was feeling sad, I was feeling anger. Someone had done this to Claire and now my brother was being blamed for it. I knew I had to do something about it. We moved over to the kitchen table and for a while, my mother and I sat in silence, eating our donuts.

"Mom, I think you should go rest," I said. She looked exhausted. I know she had been up almost as early as I had because on Black Friday there were usually guests who wanted some coffee and a to-go breakfast while they were on the way to do their shopping.

She hesitated for a moment, looking out the window. The trees in the yard were bare and it was the point in fall where everything looked brown and dead. The snow of winter was always welcomed because it covered up the barren landscape in a beautiful, sparkly cover.

I was glad to see some snowflakes in the air. If there was anything that could give us a small happiness boost, it was snow. My mother often said that no matter what month of the year it was, snow was always beautiful and I had to agree.

"It's okay Mom," I said. I reached over and held her hand. It was small and bony, a reminder that while she wasn't old yet, she was getting older. "I'll watch the desk. I think you should go lie down for a little while. Or maybe you could keep working on your plan for the holiday decorating contest. Either way, I think you need to go take a break."

She took a deep breath before nodding. We stood up together and walked out of the kitchen to the staircase. My mother went up a few stairs before coming back down and wrapping me in a big hug. We stood for a while, she and I, hugging and supporting each other both physically and emotionally.

"I love you Tessa," she said in my ear. "I'm so sorry for everything you've been through today."

"You don't have to be sorry Mom," I said. "It isn't like you caused any of this."

"I know, but as a mother you are supposed to be able to help your children and protect them from things," she said. "And today you've found a murder victim and your brother is being questioned by the police about it. I feel like I've failed you."

We were hugging so close that I couldn't see my mother's face, but her shaking voice and the wetness on my shoulder told me she was crying. I squeezed her hard, not wanting to be the first one to let go. I only stopped when I felt her arms start to loosen from around me.

My mother stepped back and put on small hand on my face. She smiled through her tears before turning to head back up the stairs. From where we were standing, I could see one of the guest rooms on the second floor had police tape across the door. That must have been where Claire was staying and the police had been fast in searching and securing it.

I headed over to the desk where I'm sure I would sit bored out of my skull for a while, but it might be good to give my brain a break. I thought about which card game I should play on the computer. I rotated between a few different ones and today I'd need to figure out which one would distract me the most.

But in the back of my mind, there was a niggling thought that I just couldn't get rid of. I wanted to figure out who did this to Claire, if only to clear my brother's name. I wanted to get into Claire's room and look around. I wanted to go back to the store to investigate. But I shouldn't do that. It wasn't my job to figure it out.

I sat down behind the ancient desktop my parents owned to keep track of bookings and guests. I pulled up the games menu and decided on good old solitaire. I opened it up and as I changed the card back picture to be a picture of Santa Claus, I decided to just try and forget about what happened that day. The police were on the case and didn't need me to interfere with their investigation. That would be easier said than done, of course.

•Chapter Nine•

A while later, I went up to my room to grab a book to read. When I moved back in with my parents, I had to move back into the only room that wasn't really taken which was my parent's library. We had our own section of the bed and breakfast that was private, just for the family. It had two bedrooms: one for my parents and another plush guest suite that Tank lived in. That left only the library to be my room. On one hand, it was nice for me because I loved to read and I was literally surrounded by books. On the other hand, it made it harder for anyone else to get a book. But I didn't plan on living with my parents forever. I just needed a bit more time to get back on my feet.

As I browsed through the shelves looking for something light to read, there was a soft knock on my door frame. I turned and saw my mother standing there. She still looked worried, but at least now she looked a little more well rested.

"How are you feeling?" I asked.

"Better," she said. "But I still haven't heard anything from your father or Tank."

That couldn't be good. I could only assume that meant they thought he was a suspect. He'd been at the station longer than I had been questioned this morning and I was the one who actually found the body.

"I'm sure we will hear from them soon," I said. I hoped that I wasn't lying to my mother. I realized that it was close to dinner time and I was sure she hadn't thought about eating. We typically ate home cooked, healthy meals, but I had another idea for this weird evening.

"Mom, I'm going to call Mike's Pizza and order us a pepperoni for delivery," I said. I knew not to ask or she would insist on making something much better for us. She nodded and went back to her bedroom to wait as I called for the pizza.

Mike's Pizza was hands down the best place to get pizza in Shady Lake. It was locally owned and had been around since my mother was in high school. In fact, her best friend had worked there at one point. Shady Lake had a couple of chain pizza stores, but Mike's was the best. Their secret was that instead of using shredded cheese, they used sliced cheese on top of their pizza. It sounds weird, but it is a total game changer.

After I made the phone call, I went down to sit in the front window and wait. When my mom came down the stairs, she stopped and looked at me for a moment before disappearing into the kitchen. She came out again holding paper plates and some forks.

"Let's eat upstairs in the family room," she said.

That was so out of character for her that it made me worry. As kids, we always begged to eat dinner in front of the television and she insisted we eat at the table. In fact, I can count on one hand the times we actually got the treat of eating in the family room.

"Okay, you go up and I'll bring the pizza when it gets here," I said.

My mom nodded and walked back up the stairs with the supplies in hand. I hoped they wouldn't take too long with the pizza because I wanted to be able to spend time with my mother. The pizza was partly my way of distracting us until we heard from Tank and my dad.

My phone buzzed as I looked out the window. I flipped it open to see a message from Clark Hutchins.

I heard that Tank was brought in. Are you and your family okay? What can I do to help?

Clark was the other man I have been casually dating. Unlike Max who was a lifelong Shady Lake resident, Clark was the handsome stranger in town. He had moved here when he took a job as a social studies teacher at Shady Lake High School.

He must have just gotten back into town from celebrating Thanksgiving and heard about everything that happened. Clark was Tank's football coach and had taught him a few times so I knew that his concern wasn't just for me, but for Tank as well.

My mom is really shaken up and my dad is there with him. They've been there all day. We don't really know what is going on. There isn't much you can do, but thank you for offering.

As I hit send, the doorbell rang. I opened it up to find a scraggly looking, long haired high school boy holding a pizza box. He shifted back and forth from one foot to the other as I handed him the money and took the pizza. The kid stood there a little longer, looking like he wanted to say something.

"You can keep the change," I said, thinking he wanted to make sure of the reason I had given him the amount of cash I had.

"Thanks," he said, continuing to stand on the front porch nervously looking around.

I looked at him for a moment before I grabbed the door and started to close it in his face. I wasn't really sure what else to do. The boy put his hand up on the door to stop me from shutting it.

"Um, by the way, I know Tank and I know he would never do something like that," the pizza boy said. He looked all around the porch, but not at me. "He's a good guy."

"Thank you," I said. Even though bad news travels fast in a small town, so do well wishes.

The boy stood there for another moment before turning, carefully descending the stairs and getting back into his rusty old car with a giant sticker for

Mike's Pizza on the side of it. As he rumbled out of the driveway, I shut the door and headed upstairs.

My mother had settled herself onto the couch they had bought last year, pulled a knitted blanket over her lap, and turned on the television. None of us watched much television, but she had picked a station that played old sitcoms so the laugh track was going full-force as I came in. It was oddly comforting.

I put a slice of pizza on each plate for us and handed one to my mom before sitting down next to her. As I bit into the greasy, cheesy slice of pizza, I promised myself that I would make a New Year's resolution to eat better. If I kept it up with the donuts and pizza, my already tight pants weren't going to button soon.

My mother's phone rang and she grabbed it off of the coffee table so fast I almost didn't see her hand shoot out from the blanket. Her face went pale as she looked at who was calling. I knew that meant it was something to do with Tank. She hit the button to answer and lifted it to her face.

"Hi honey, how is he doing? Uh huh. But he won't say where he was that night? They can't hold him very long, can they? That long? Really? Well let me know when you know more."

She hit the end button and put her phone back on the table as her hand shook. I had been hungry for another slice of pizza, but now I wasn't so sure.

"That was your father," she said. "He said that he and Tank are still going to be there for a while. Apparently they can hold a suspect for quite a while if they are suspected of something as bad as murder and Tank says he was busy Thanksgiving night, but won't actually give his alibi."

She started to softly cry and I leaned over to give her a hug. I wished I could give my dad a hug too. I can't imagine how hard it is to sit in and listen to your son be questioned as a suspect in such a heinous murder.

I couldn't believe the police still wanted to hold him. They really had nothing against him besides the facts that he had a key to the store, is big enough to have actually physically done it, and for some reason won't provide an alibi. I had to admit it looked fishy, but there were no clues actually tying him to the scene.

But when small town cops have something big like this happen, they tend to jump to a conclusion and then develop tunnel vision to anything else. I don't have anything against the cops. Heck, I'm dating one. But they weren't used to big investigations and I think they get a little too excited when they have to do one.

We went back to watching the television for a while. A man and a woman were involved in some sort of slapstick routine where they were trying to pack a suitcase to go on vacation but they couldn't quite get it shut. It was funny, but I just couldn't bring myself to laugh at it. The humor paled somewhat in comparison to the real life situation we were dealing with.

"Tessa, could you do something for me?" my mother said quietly once the end credits started to roll. "I don't really want to ask you. In fact your father would absolutely kill me if he knew I was asking you."

"What is it?" I said. I put my hand on her arm. She often looked much younger than her fifty-five years, but right now she looked older. The day had really taken a toll on her.

"I need you to look into this situation and find something so that we can prove Tank had nothing to do with it," my mom said. "You are so good at solving these things. Now I need you to solve this. You don't need to interfere with the investigation, We just need something small that will point them in a different direction. I'm counting on you."

I took a second slice of pizza and thought about it for a moment. Obviously I wanted to help my family, especially my brother. But I wasn't really a detective. I've stumbled my way through a murder investigation before and I like to listen to true crime podcasts. I still don't have any training or anything though. How in the world was I going to do this?

"I'll do it," I said. I didn't really have a choice. I needed to get Tank out of there.

•Chapter Ten•

The first thing I needed to do was to get back into the Christmas Shop and look for clues. But I couldn't ask Sue for help. As much as I believed she didn't do this, she was a suspect. I didn't want to ask a suspect for help because I'd accidentally done that before and it had almost gotten me shot.

My mother and I had stayed up almost all night watching old sitcoms together on the couch because neither of us could go to sleep. We had changed into our pajamas and gotten ready for bed but both of us had drifted back to the couch, hoping we would hear Tank and my dad coming in.

Once it hit four in the morning, I called Mandy and asked if I could help her make donuts. She was bright and peppy and agreed immediately to my help, although I was a terrible baker and didn't provide much actual help. After changing into a pair of jeans and an older top that I knew would be covered in flour by the time I was done, I headed towards the Donut Hut.

When I walked into the familiar warmth, Mandy was chipper as always. She had a carafe of coffee and a mug ready for me as she was busily frosting donuts. She smiled as I walked in and hung my jacket before pouring myself a cup of coffee. I had text her the night before, so she knew what was happening with Tank and she knew that this was another situation where I needed a little time before I'd talk.

I drank the first cup of coffee fast and was distracted enough by pouring myself another that I hadn't noticed Mandy had warmed up a breakfast sandwich for me. I thanked her before taking a big bite. Then I told her all of the details that I knew about the murder and the investigation. When I was done, she stopped frosting and looked up at me.

"And now you want to go looking for your own clues, right?" she asked. She knew me too well.

"Yes," I said, hanging my head a bit. "But only because my own mother asked me to. She is so distraught over Tank being a suspect and she wants me to find something to get the police to look the other way."

"I hate to tell you, but that will be sort of hard to do," she said as she artfully added sprinkles to the donuts. "Trevor said the police are not really investigating any other suspects, at least as far as he can tell."

Trevor is Mandy's boyfriend and not only is he an emergency dispatcher, but he also is pretty good friends with several of the police officers in town. To me, the fact that he has a steady job is about his only redeeming factor. I've never quite understood what

Mandy sees in him, but they've been together for over a decade now and live together above the Donut Hut.

"I don't suppose there is any way you can come with me to the Christmas Shop, right?" I asked. I really needed backup, but I also didn't want to make Mandy lose track of everything she needed to do. The Donut Hut was run on a shoestring budget, just barely making enough to keep afloat and make sure Mandy could pay all of her bills. I didn't want to do anything that may endanger that, including getting her wrapped up in a murder investigation.

"I figured you were going to ask," she said. "Let me pop one more tray in the oven and then I'll have a chunk of time to come with while they bake."

I put my jacket on and once she put the tray in, I handed her jacket to her. She set a timer on her phone for fifteen minutes so that we didn't lost track of time and we popped out the door into the cold.

When we got to the Christmas Shop, I looked around and besides the police tape that was still over the door, no one was around. If the police really thought they had their suspect in custody, I really doubted they'd have anyone watching the store.

"I'm going to go in and investigate something I saw the other day when I found Claire," I said. "You stand here and let me know if you see anything."

I handed her one of my heavy duty flashlights. I had made sure to grab an extra before I went to the

Donut Hut. I had my regular flashlight from my purse and an older digital camera in my other hand. The one thing that wasn't great about a flip phone was that even if you got one with a camera, it did not have great resolution. If I found anything, I needed to be able to take pictures to show the police.

I snuck in the front door, careful to open the door slowly so that the bell would not chime loudly. It was funny, I was almost positive there would be no one there, but I still wanted to make sure to be quiet. I guess that might be colored by the fact that the last time I came and thought no one was here, I found a murder scene.

The aisles were still exactly how we had left them, still all ready to have a grand opening that I feared would never come. The police hadn't made too big of a mess, so I was hopeful that the shop could open as soon as they were done with the investigation.

I made my way over to the aisle where I had found Claire's body. It had been cleaned up and besides an outline on the floor where she had been found, you couldn't tell there had been a murder there. I shone my flashlight around the aisle, looking for that glint of gold I had noticed before. It might not even be related to the murder, but I just wanted to see what it was.

When I finally spotted the shimmer, I dropped

to my knees and crawled towards it, careful not to touch anything. I lay the flashlight down on the ground so it gave light at a good angle. I pulled out my camera and started to snap pictures. It was a little gold wire charm, like you would find on a bracelet. It was shaped like a little horse. I tried to think if I had seen a charm bracelet on Claire. It didn't seem like the sort of thing she would have worn, but I was definitely basing that on the stereotype of suburban women I knew and not on the ten minutes I had actually met her.

I closed my eyes and tried to flashback to see if I had noticed her wearing any sort of jewelry, but I just couldn't. The only thing I remembered was that she was wearing all black. For one split second, I wondered if Sue had any sort of security camera before I remembered that usually this space was a second hand store and probably didn't need that sort of thing around.

"Psst, Tessa?" Mandy's voice cut through the quiet darkness.

"Is someone coming?" I asked frantically. I scrambled to my feet and grabbed the flashlight off of the ground. I did not want to get caught inside of a crime scene. My mother did not need a second child to be hauled in for questioning under suspicion of being a murderer.

"No, but my phone timer went off," she said. "I

67

need to get back to the bakery right now so that I can get the donuts out before they burn."

"Okay, I'm coming," I said.

I quickly flipped through my pictures to make sure I had enough and then I scurried towards the front door. Mandy was waiting impatiently out front in the cold. She deserved an extra nice Christmas gift from me this year. I nodded at her as I shut the door to the Christmas Shop and together we ran through the streets back to the Donut Hut. I hadn't been that worried about being caught inside, but I was quite aware how suspicious we looked, running through the dark streets of Shady Lake carrying flashlights in the early morning.

As we reached the bakery, I knew that my next step was to figure out where that charm had come from. I'd have to enlist help from Max to try and figure it out, but I also knew I'd probably have to trick him into it. Max was an upstanding police officer who did everything he could to not jeopardize investigations, even for me. But maybe I could use my feminine wiles to get him to give up a little information to me.

•Chapter Eleven•

I was glad that I had been able to get Max to come out for breakfast with me, but ordering pancakes had been a mistake. We were at a Shady Lake staple restaurant called The Breakfast Spot and they were known for their pancakes. Well actually, what you got was one pancake so large that it covered your entire plate. Any side dishes came on separate little plates. The secret to eating it is to cut a hole in the middle. That's where you put your syrup and then you eat the pancake from the inside out.

But I had eaten way too many donuts in the last two days so I'm not sure why I thought I'd want a sweet pancake, even if it is the most delicious pancake in the entire world. Looking around, I spotted someone who ordered a more sensible breakfast of eggs, hash browns, and sausage. But there was only the one person as every single other person was having a pancake.

Max had also ordered a pancake, but he had upgraded it to a bananas foster pancake which meant that the plate sized pancake had been piled high with sliced bananas, caramel sauce, and whipped cream. It was basically like having dessert for breakfast. Even my sweet tooth wasn't sure how he could eat the entire thing, but I also know he hadn't eaten at least a half dozen donuts in the last two days like I had.

The Breakfast Spot was unusual as all of the cooking was done in the center of the restaurant. There was a big griddle where all of the pancakes and other things were made. The cook and the wait staff bustled around the little rectangle cooking and pouring coffee. Around the rectangular kitchen area was a breakfast bar with big, pleather round barstools. This was where the regulars sat. All of the regulars were retired men who met each morning to read the newspaper, eat breakfast, and chat about the goings on of the world. Most were lifelong Shady Lake residents and the rest had been here long enough to be considered lifelong residents.

The outer loop of the restaurant was lined with booths and pictures of local things hung on the walls. There were team pictures, both current and older. There were also pictures of Shady Lake when it first became a town hanging above several booths. The people who owned The Breakfast Spot had so many historical pictures that they swapped them around monthly so that it felt like there was always something new to look at and read, even if you always sat at the same table.

Each booth could comfortably seat at least six people and some were even bigger. This is where everyone else sat because if you came to The Breakfast Spot, you came with a group. There were families and groups of high school kids all eating breakfast. It was warm and bustling.

I made sure to have us meet as the breakfast rush at The Breakfast Spot was dying down. They only served breakfast, but they stayed open until lunchtime so that people could sit and relax and enjoy their breakfasts slowly. Most tables were finishing up their meals as we were just getting ours. Once the tables around us were a bit scarce, I decided to make my move.

"Was Claire wearing a charm bracelet when she was taken in?" I asked casually as I cut another piece of pancake.

"You know I can't talk about the case," Max said, shooting me a confused and disapproving look. I knew full well, which is why I hadn't technically asked him about the case. And I told him so.

"I didn't ask about her murder, I simply asked if she had been wearing a bracelet," I said.

Max took a big bite of his bananas foster pancake. I could tell he was weighing that back and forth in his mind. Max and I had dated seriously for years in high school, so he knew me almost as well as Mandy did. He knew I had some sort of plan in the works, but he just couldn't figure out exactly what it was.

I casually took some sips of my coffee as I waited. Finally, he swallowed a big gulp and nodded his head.

"Yes, she was wearing a charm bracelet," he said carefully. "Now tell me why you wanted to know."

I pulled my camera out of my bag and pulled up the first picture I had taken. It was a wide shot showing both the outline where her body had been and the glint from under the shelves next to it.

"Because I found one of her charms that was hiding under the shelf and had not been collected by you guys," I said. "Don't worry, I left it there and I didn't touch it. I just took pictures."

I scrolled to the next picture and then the next. Max's face dropped into a surprised confusion and he grabbed the camera out of my hands. As he scrolled through the pictures, I could see him mouthing some expletives that I pretended not to notice. I sipped my coffee and waited for him to look up from the camera.

"Tessa, I've told you before that you can't just go wandering around a crime scene," he started in. "And I'm going to have to take this memory card."

"Why?" I asked. "You should go to the store and get the charm instead."

Max whispered another expletive. He rarely swore, so he must have really been upset with himself. It wasn't really his fault if something got missed, though. He wasn't that high in the chain of command and he was a loyal officer who did what he was told to do. I reached across the table and took his hand.

"I told you this so that you could get it and maybe swab it for some DNA," I said. "I'm hoping it will show that Tank was not the one who did this."

"I know, Tessa," he said, giving my hand a squeeze. "And I hope you know that I am trying my hardest to find something to help get the focus off of Tank. I've known Tank his entire life and I know he wouldn't do this, but I do wish he would make it a little easier by giving us his alibi. He says he was busy and that there are people who could corroborate for him, but he won't actually tell us what he was doing."

My stomach had settled a little bit, so I ate another bite of pancake while I thought about it. What in the world could he have been doing that he doesn't want to tell people? I don't think it would be anything illegal. Hopefully they would release Tank soon and I could get his alibi out of him in case the police circled back around to him.

A faint ringing could be heard as I took a drink of coffee. I looked around, wondering whose phone it was. Suddenly, I realized it was my phone. I must have bumped the ringer this time. The hot coffee scalded my throat as I tried to swallow it quickly so I could answer. I flipped it open and saw that my mother was calling.

"Tessa, I don't want you to freak out, but I am

73

in an ambulance on the way to the hospital," she said.

"What? What happened?" I said, a little too loudly as the people around me looked our way in concern. I mouthed an apology to them.

"I'm okay, but I fell and I think I broke my leg," she said. "That darn ice patch on the front porch got me."

I made a mental note to go buy a big rubber mat to put over it as I said goodbye and hung up. I filled Max in on what happened and he flagged the waitress down to get me a cup of coffee to go. As I frantically tried to get my jacket on, Max stood up and put his hands on my shoulders to calm me down. He looked me in the eyes and smiled before taking my jacket and helping me into it one arm at a time.

"It will be okay," Max said. "Everything will get figured out; your mom's leg, Tank, everything will be fine."

Somehow when Max said that, I believed him. Maybe it was the comfortable familiarity or maybe deep down I truly believed that also. He leaned forward and gave me a quick peck on the lips. He didn't like to show much public affection, but I knew the love behind the kiss was what mattered.

As I started the station wagon in the parking lot, I wondered what in the world Tank could have been doing that night. I filed that question away with all of the other things I wanted to investigate and headed towards the hospital to find my mother.

•Chapter Twelve•

I was sitting in one of the emergency room bays with the curtain drawn around it waiting for the nurse to bring my mother back from getting a cast put on her leg when I realized something. I had been so wrapped up in finding the body and then trying to figure out the whole Tank thing that I never tried to figure out why Claire was at the Christmas Shop that night in the first place.

Would she have been there to try and cause mayhem and make the store fail so that Sue would have to shut it down? If she was trying to do that, she hadn't done it very well because everything was still neat and orderly on the shelves, so much so that we hadn't even noticed anything different about the store until we spotted her body.

Was she expecting to meet someone there? The neat and orderly shelves didn't suggest much of a struggle, so I assumed she hadn't been caught totally off guard by the presence of another person there.

My thoughts wandered again to Sue. Maybe she had been the one to do it. It was her store, her livelihood that she stood to lose and her keys were in the door. Normally Sue was very mild-mannered, but when everything was on the line, who could blame her for being angry? I just couldn't figure out how small, sweet, frail Sue would have mustered enough physical strength to stab someone with a Christmas ornament even if she was filled with rage and adrenaline.

I needed to clear my head a bit and get some of these thoughts down on paper. I grabbed my purse and rifled around inside. I found a ballpoint pen, but somehow in a purse big enough to carry a large, heavy flashlight, I didn't have any paper besides a few old receipts.

I made my way to the nurse's station across the hallway from where I was waiting and asked if they had some pieces of paper I could have. The busy nurse shoved an entire pad of paper at me without responding before answering the phone and punching in some numbers on the computer. I thanked her and she gave a little wave of her hand before going back to typing things.

At the top of the paper, I wrote SUSPECTS and then I made two columns, one labeled PRO, meaning the motive and anything implicating them, and the other labeled CON, or anything that mean they couldn't have done it. Then I wrote Sue's name and everything I had been thinking of: her motive, her small stature, everything.

The next person I put was Tank. It pained me to even think about my sweet baby brother being a murder suspect, but if I was going to solve this case I needed to think like the police were thinking. Under PRO, I wrote that he would lose his job, he had threatened Claire and that he was big enough to have actually committed the crime. I didn't have anything to write under CON yet, so I just left it blank, but I drew a little heart to show that I loved him and knew he didn't do it.

The other person who had threatened Claire was Rich, so he was next on my list. I wrote that he had also been angry with her and physically, he also could have hurt Claire. But besides that threat, why would he want to hurt her? I would need to dive a little deeper with Rich to try and figure out why he had felt so passionately about Claire's plan to shut down the Used-A-Bit. I had an inkling that it had to do with Sue.

The only other person besides me who had been there when Claire came was Jill. I wrote her name down. Her motive was that she didn't want to live above a dog grooming shop. But I questioned whether she was actually strong enough to have done the crime.

As I tapped my pen on my paper and tried to think a little bit more about the murder and any other suspects, the curtains were pushed open and my mother appeared sitting in a wheelchair. I quickly folded the paper and shoved it in my purse. I didn't need my mother to worry any more about Tank or the crime. Right now I just needed to get her home.

I handed my mother her jacket as I slipped mine on and grabbed both of our purses. The nurse told me to run ahead and pull the car up so we didn't have to walk through the cold so I did, making sure to put a blanket on the cold, leather passenger seat and cranking up the heat. At the door, the nurse helped my mother into the car and gave a friendly wave as we pulled out of the drop-off zone.

I stole a glance at my mother. She looked older and even more tired, exhausted from both the accident and still not knowing anything about how Tank was doing. She had her head leaned back on the headrest and her eyes were shut. The painkiller hadn't worn off yet, but I knew that I'd have to go fill her prescription once we got home and got her settled. I wasn't actually sure how I was going to get her inside and up all of those icy stairs, but we would figure it out together.

"Tessa, I just thought of something else," my mom said. "How am I going to finish my decorating for the contest? I have such a good plan this year and I will finally be able to get our house featured, I just know it."

"I'll do it Mom," I said. "I'm sure Trina, Tilly, and Teddy will help me. I think with your plan and our muscles, we can win this thing. Why don't we drive around for a little inspiration?"

The absence of Tank's name in that list hung in the air. I didn't know what to say, so I stayed quiet for a moment. Then I reached over and turned on the radio to Shady Lake's AM station. They had started playing their holiday playlist, which brightened the mood a bit.

We drove through Shady Lake and while I wanted to get my mother home, the car was so warm and cozy that I took the long way. There was just a faint dusting of snow on the ground. It was just enough to make all of the Christmas decorations really stand out and sparkle. I was hoping the little detour through some of the holiday things would cheer my mom up a bit. If nothing else, I knew it would cheer me up a bit.

I made sure to drive past some of the previous winners of the decorating contest to see if they had any decorations up yet, but everyone seemed to be playing it pretty close to the vest. Mostly what we saw was very basic light displays. It was like most people were waiting to put up the really flashy stuff until it was too late to be replicated.

When I pulled into the driveway, I right away noticed my father's car parked in the usual spot. I wasn't sure if that meant Tank was home or not, but I decided to be optimistic. I knew I'd need help getting my mom up the stairs and into the house so I told her to hold tight as I went to get someone.

As I bounded up the stairs, the front door flew open and Tank came running out with my dad close behind him. He had a wide smile on his face, so wide that if he smiled any more, it would crack his face wide open.

"Tank, what are you doing home?" I yelled as I ran into his giant bear hug.

"They let me go," he said. "And the good news is that they found more evidence that points to a different suspect so I am completely off the hook. Apparently they went back to the store and found some more stuff. We wanted to surprise you and Mom. Where were you anyways?"

Apparently the bad news had not reached them yet. I nodded my head towards the car and beckoned them to follow me around to the passenger side. Tank gave my mom the news through the window she had cranked open. My mom's face was absolutely jubilant when Tank came up to her window and gave her the good news.

"Why don't you get out of the car and we can celebrate Mom?" Tank said.

My mom grimaced and pointed down towards her leg. My dad and Tank competed for space as they both leaned into the car to look. At the sight of the large cast, they both yelled in surprise and concern.

After a short explanation, the men worked together to carry my mother inside and upstairs to our family room where we settled her in on the couch and arranged a late lunch for everyone. I warmed our leftover pizza up in the oven and while most of it was scarfed up by Tank, there was enough for both of my parents to have some too. I just had coffee as my stomach was still full from my pancake breakfast.

This day had been full of twists and turns and it was only lunchtime. Who knew the holiday season could be so suspenseful? And no one had even been arrested yet.

•Chapter Thirteen•

"So tell me what happened," I said once Tank had slowed down his lunch inhalation.

"I don't really know," he said with a shrug. "They had been questioning me for so long and they kept asking me the same things over and over again. The police were starting to get a little angry with me because they were convinced it was me and that I was just holding out on them. Then all of a sudden they came back from one of their breaks and told me things had changed and that I could go. They told me to stick around town, but that I was no longer considered a suspect."

I thought back to the Christmas Shop as I had seen it early that morning and wondered what else they had found. What did I miss that would have ruled Tank out? I don't think they could have tested any DNA on that charm that fast. I would have to try to get some information out of Max.

"Well no matter what, I'm just glad to have you home," my mom said quietly. She grabbed Tank's large hand in her small bony one. "I'm just sorry that I'll need to ask you to do some extra help around here."

"Oh yes," I said. "We are going to need to get the B&B ready for the holiday decorating contest soon. The judging is less than a week away and we haven't done anything yet. Well, Mom has done some planning, but we need to do the actual decorating now."

"Well I'm kind of busy, but I can help out a bit," Tank said, shifting around in his seat a bit. I remembered that he wouldn't give his alibi and I wondered what he was hiding. I needed to try and ask him about it.

"First order of business is for Mom to tell us her vision," I announced. "Dad, why don't you fetch her planning materials while Tank and I take the dishes downstairs."

My mom started describing where all of her planning papers were while Tank grabbed some dirty plates and I grabbed the baking tray where the pizza had been. We walked downstairs without talking, but once we walked through the kitchen's swinging doors I took my chance.

"What are you doing that is keeping you so busy lately?" I asked. I tried to be nonchalant about it as I squirted dish soap on the baking tray and scrubbed off the stuck on crust bits. I glanced briefly at Tank's face to try to get a read on his feelings, but it was pretty neutral. I didn't blame him; he was probably exhausted after all of the questioning he had been through.

"I just have a lot of things on my plate," he said

as he loaded the dishwasher. I couldn't tell if he was blushing a little bit or if he was just tired.

As I scrubbed, I made a quick decision to push on with my questions. I decided that he must be blushing and there was only one thing that would make a teenage boy blush: his family trying to figure out his love life.

"Is it a girlfriend?" I asked. "Have you been meeting up with a girl?"

"Not meeting up with a girl, no," he said. The way he said it was very particular.

"But does it involve a girl?"

"Sort of."

"Is it a girl who can give you an alibi if you need it again?"

"No," Tank said. He turned to face me, his face a bit cloudy. "She isn't my girlfriend, not yet anyways. But I won't tell you anything else unless you promise not to tell anyone. Not the cops. Not Mom and Dad. No one."

I weighed that back and forth while I grabbed a dish towel to dry the baking sheet. I didn't like to make promises I couldn't keep and I wasn't sure I'd be able to keep it to myself if the police did come for him again and I knew his alibi.

But I looked at his face. I could see that he was desperate to tell someone and to have someone he knew he could trust. I may have to work hard at not letting my big mouth run the show, but I decided it was worth it to be my brother's secret keeper.

"Okay, I promise," I said. I stuck out my pinky finger towards him. The Schmidt siblings take pinky promises very seriously and we always have, although Tank and I had enough of an age difference that we hardly ever made them together.

But Tank locked his large pinky around my thin one and gave it a firm shake. He walked over to the kitchen table and sat down. I poured myself another cup of coffee and followed him over.

"There is this girl at school," he said. "Her name is Angie and she just moved here like a month ago. Anyway, she's really cool and I like her a lot and I think she likes me too. But I don't know how to ask her out."

"That can be tricky," I said. I practically had to sit on my hands to stop myself from squealing and jumping up and down. As a typical teenage boy, Tank played his love life close, never telling us much of anything about it. I continued to sip my coffee, playing it cool so that he would hopefully tell me more.

"I think she likes me," he said. "Actually I know she likes me but I just didn't know what to do about it. But last week, we were hanging out and she was talking about how she wanted a nice guitar so bad but that her parents wouldn't be able to afford one. So I decided that I was going to buy her one and then maybe ask her if she wanted to go out with me."

I was a bit taken aback by how romantic Tank was. For someone who was literally built like a Tank, he was a soft teddy bear inside.

"So I looked at some guitars at the music shop downtown and they had a purple one that I think Angie would love because her favorite color is purple," he continued. "But it is super expensive and I knew I wouldn't be able to buy it just from what I was making at the Christmas Shop. So I went out to get another job. I wanted something where I knew I could make some good money but that it wouldn't interfere with school or working at the Christmas Shop."

"Wait, you went out and got a second job?" I asked. I had not seen that coming. When the topic of Angie had come come up, I figured he was just spending time with her.

"Yeah, I had an idea to talk to some of the local bar owners and ask if they needed someone to do the clean up. They pretty much all took me up on it, so after bar close I go in and clean everything up. The only thing is I'm underage so technically I'm not supposed to work anywhere that serves alcohol. So they all pay me under the table and I can't tell anyone about it or they will get in trouble."

Well this was all starting to make a weird sort of sense. He couldn't tell the police that or both he and the bar owners would get in legal trouble. He also couldn't tell my parents that. My parents weren't against drinking or the local bars, but I was pretty sure they would be a bit upset about their teenage son working there.

"But if I can keep it all up, I'll be able to buy her that guitar in another couple of weeks," Tank said. He was staring starry-eyed out the window. I had never met Angie, but I had to imagine she was beautiful if she did this to my giant of a brother. "She plays guitar and sings so beautifully. I can't wait to see her play that purple guitar."

"I promise not to tell Mom and Dad," I said. "But you have to promise me something. After you give her that guitar, you need to introduce her to me. I'd love to hear her play that guitar."

Tank smiled at me. Sometimes I forgot how old he actually was. When I thought of my baby brother, he always seemed to be perpetually four years old. But here he was holding down two jobs while going to school and wooing a girl. I guess I'd have to get my subconscious to update his perpetual age.

"We should probably get back upstairs," Tank said, suddenly embarrassed by our previous conversation.

He quickly stood up and headed towards the door. As I stood up with my coffee cup, my phone buzzed in my pocket. I promised Tank I'd be up in a moment and checked my message. It was from Max.

Thanks for the tip today Sweet Thing.

I couldn't help but smile. I decided I'd try to kill two birds with one stone and invite him over.

You're welcome :) Are you busy? I need to help my mom start to decorate for the contest and I could use a little help.

Max told me he didn't have anything planned and told me he'd be over in an hour or so, dressed to help outside. The chilly November wind was blowing and could cut through a person if they weren't wearing enough layers.

After I went upstairs, I was glad I had asked for his help. My mother's plans were ambitious and I would need as much help as I could get, especially if I also had to take over inside decorating, gift buying, gift wrapping, and planning our holiday meal.

•Chapter Fourteen•

Ten strands of Christmas lights had not been near enough for my mother's ambitious plans. As Max and I worked on getting them on the house, I had sent my father and Tank to the store in my station wagon to buy more. The first part of the plan was simply to outline the entire house with lights. On an old, three-story Victorian style house, that equaled a very long length of Christmas lights.

We had started on the third level of the house and worked our way down. Thankfully my parents had an extendable ladder that we could use to reach that high, but it made me nervous. Max had no problem getting up there, though. He had always been a thrill seeker.

Technically Max shouldn't even be helping as he was part of the judging committee but he said as long as he was only helping with the very basic lights and not the other stuff, it wouldn't be a problem. Besides, it wasn't like he was the only cop with personal ties to one of the entrants of the light contest. That was one of the perils of being in a small town.

As Max reached the end of the last strand of lights we had, Max climbed back down the ladder and plopped down in one of the wicker chairs on the front porch. I sat down in the one next to him and smiled as he put his hand on my knee. Thankfully the wind had died down and we were protected from what little breeze there was here on the porch.

"So Tank is no longer a suspect?" I said as casually as I could as I pulled out the thermos of coffee my father kept refilling for us. I poured two cups of steaming hot coffee and handed Max the mug that said BAH HUMBUG on it.

"No, he isn't," Max said in a measured tone.

"And you have a new suspect?" I asked casually.

Max took a sip of coffee and I did the same, trying not to gulp it down in my excitement over both a hot beverage and the fact that Max may answer my questions about their investigation.

"We do have a new suspect," he said. "And I will tell you more about it only because you have done a lot of legwork and it'll be in the news soon enough. Chelsea was there when we got him to the courthouse, so it will be on the front page of the paper tomorrow."

"Well, who was it?"

"Rich," Max said.

"Rich?!?" I blurted out. "What did you find to implicate him?"

"I shouldn't be telling you this, but I'd much rather you knew than Chelsea," Max said, rolling his eyes. I could just imagine her badgering them as they brought Rich into the jailhouse in handcuffs. "When we were looking for the charm that you told me about, we noticed cigar ash under the lip of the shelves. And we all know Rich likes a good cigar."

I sat back in the chair and looked out over the frozen lake while I thought about that. The lake wasn't frozen through yet, but soon enough it would be and the view would be dotted with ice houses and snowmobiles. I liked to enjoy it now when it was icy and snow covered but no one had invaded it yet.

Rich had definitely been on my suspect list so that wasn't totally out of left field. But I didn't think it would really matter if there was a dog grooming salon next to his bar, so that couldn't be the full motive. I did have to kind of kick myself for missing the cigar ash. I had just been so distracted by the charm I found.

"Okay, so if Rich was the one that killed Claire, what was he doing in the store?" I asked.

"Our working theory is that he happened to see her going into the Christmas Shop to do some mischief as he was closing up the Loony Bin," Max said. "We think that it made him so mad that he went in and the confrontation drove him into a fit of rage."

"You think Old Man Rich was driven into a fit of rage by Claire?" I said. That just didn't make sense to me. "Sure, he was mad about what Claire said when she was there before, but I don't think he was mad enough to confront her and then subsequently kill her."

"Well, I said it was a working theory," Max said. "We aren't exactly sure yet, but we just know that he did it. Rich said he was busy that night, but he won't tell us what he was doing. Apparently that is a running theme during this investigation. Maybe he and Tank were somewhere together."

As Max chuckled, I just about blurted out that I knew where Tank had been, but I pressed my lips together and then swallowed down more coffee. I couldn't spill his secret, especially not less than a few hours after Tank had told it to me. Instead I just shrugged as I tried to slurp down more coffee without burning my mouth and esophagus.

"Rich says he wasn't alone, but that he would rather not say who he was with," Max said, rolling his eyes. "I told him that was not how an alibi works. But he is remaining steadfast that he doesn't want to say."

I filed that away, telling myself I would think about how to figure out his alibi later. Maybe I would ask Sue. She and Rich seemed pretty close. That reminded me to ask Max one more important question.

"So if you think you are mostly done with the investigation, then I'd like to know when the Christmas Shop will be able to open," I said. "You know we still haven't had our grand opening yet and it would be nice to do that before Christmas is actually here."

"I actually called Sue right before I came here," Max said with a laugh. "I told her to give us tomorrow to go through the shop one more time to make sure we didn't miss anything else and that she would be good to go for a grand opening any time next week."

I smiled at him and patted his hand in thanks. Hopefully we could still get people to come out despite the murder that had happened in the shop. I made a mental note to call Sue later so we could plan this grand opening.

The station wagon came rolling into the driveway with Tank in the front seat pumping his fists into the air like some sort of champion. The entire back end looked like it was full of boxes of lights. I had to laugh as he jumped out and yelled up to us.

"We literally just bought them out of lights," he said. "We bought like fifty strands of lights."

"I figured that any we didn't use on the house could be used on some of the trees," my dad said with a shrug. My father was a frugal man, but one thing he wasn't afraid to spend money on was my mother. If she wanted something, he would buy it for her and make sure it was top of the line. If my mother wanted the house decorated for the holidays, then by golly he

94

was going to decorate it as much as he possibly could.

As Max drained his coffee cup and then went down to help unload the car, I thought about what he had told me. I hadn't seen it coming that Rich would be killer. Sure, he had been upset at Claire, but so had the rest of us. And although I had only met her that once, I was pretty sure she wasn't the type of person who endeared people to her.

For now, though, I had to push all of that out of my mind. I had fifty more strands of lights to help organize and hang up and we were running out of daylight. I also had to figure out if Rich actually had an alibi and plan the grand opening of the Christmas Shop on top of doing all of the holiday preparations my mother normally did. I wondered if I'd get any time to relax before the new year because so far it wasn't looking like it.

•Chapter Fifteen•

We had done as much work as we could on the house decorations until the sun had set on us. Then we had sent Max out to pick up some Chinese food for us. Any significant others of us Schmidt children quickly figured out that they would be hazed upon joining the family in the form of light teasing and being sent out on errands. As I waited for Max to get back, I realized why Tank would be tentative about introducing us to Angie.

I had also sent a quick message to Sue who assured me she would come over the next day to do some planning with me. I was a little surprised she hadn't been the one to contact me, but it had been so crazy lately that I didn't really blame her.

The next day, Sue came over to have lunch while we got our planning done. I had whipped up some quick sandwiches with a side salad. I knew my stomach could use some vegetables after all of the junk food I had been ingesting.

Unfortunately, it was Sunday so we either would need to wait an entire week to have the grand opening on a weekend or we would just have to do it on a weekday, so I had quickly jotted down two plans before she arrived. If we were going to open on a weekday, we may as well do it tomorrow so the one plan was for the grand opening to happen quickly. If we waited until the weekend, we would have more time and could make it bigger. So the other plan was for a bigger and better opening. I figured she could just pick one and we could go for it.

"I am a little worried, Tessa," Sue said. "What if people don't want to come out to the store now? If we wait until next weekend, people might not want to buy any more decorations. They may be done shopping by then. But I want to make sure the grand opening is a success. How can we make both of those things happen?"

I speared a tomato and thought about it for a moment before an idea struck. I put up a finger telling Sue to wait while I jumped out of my chair. We kept flyers with the going-ons around the town up at the desk. I tried to quickly chew up my mouthful of food as I rushed back to the table with a copy of the flyer.

"Could we wait until Wednesday and do our grand opening then?" I asked as I shoved the flyer under her nose. "Wednesday is the Downtown Shady Lake Holiday Shopping Night."

Sue read the flyer a few times with a blank look on her face as I tried not to make excited noises. After a moment, she set it down and looked at me.

"I can't believe I forgot about this," she said, gesturing to the flyer. "That is a great idea Tessa. We could do the grand opening at six when people are out and about shopping. Hopefully the ribbon cutting will draw people over."

"I can believe you forgot it," I said. "You've had some bigger things on your mind than that. But I think that will be perfect. Hold on a minute and I will try to mesh these two plans together."

We ate in silence for a bit while I combined plans for the quick grand opening and the big grand opening together. It was like the best of both worlds and I hoped that it would make up for the event that had derailed the first grand opening.

Once I had the plan written down, I went to the kitchen to grab us both a slice of apple pie that we had leftover from Thanksgiving. I was hoping it would entice Sue to eat a bit more. She had just picked at her lunch and while I was sure she was still pretty shaken up by the murder, I also knew that she was so skinny that she couldn't stand to lose any weight.

I sat down and took a few bites of the warmed pie with whipped cream before I started to explain my plan to her. I had previously worked in marketing, so I told her I would come up with a short-term marketing plan if she would agree to some sort of grand opening sale. Sue nodded and agreed to figure out a good sale. I was just hoping I wouldn't have to talk to Chelsea at the newspaper. She thrived on the crime beat and would want to spin the whole story to be about the murder instead of about the holiday store.

Then I told Sue my other ideas for the opening. I knew that one of the high school choirs was performing at the shopping event and I said I would talk to the director to see if they could perform a special song in front of the store. We also had at least two strands of lights leftover from the house decorating and I knew I could use them to decorate her windows a bit more. I would jazz up the window displays.

Throughout my explanation, Sue nodded along and looked like she was listening, but the twinkle in her eye was gone. When she first came up with the idea for the Christmas Shop, she had been so excited that she practically danced when she talked about it. Her eyes twinkled merrily and you could just see her passion.

But now her eyes were dull and lifeless. I wasn't sure if Sue had just taken the entire situation really hard or if there was something else going on. I wouldn't blame her if she had been hit really hard. After all, someone had been murdered in her shop. That is a pretty big deal.

After I finished telling her the plan, I sat back and waited for her to give her input. She ate a few more bites of her apple pie and I was pleased to see she had eaten nearly the entire slice while I had rambled on. That was a good sign.

"I think that is a great plan Tessa," Sue said. "I'm so glad you have agreed to help me. I don't know what I would do without you."

"Well don't worry, I'm going to be here with you through the holiday season," I said, even though I wasn't exactly sure how I was supposed to get everything done. I would just have to manage. At some points in life, you just get through and the next couple of weeks would be one of those times for me.

We wrapped up a few final details, writing down what each of us would need to do. Then, we agreed to meet the next day to update each other and decide on the next steps. We would need to work really hard to get everything ready, but Sue didn't have anyone else to help her.

When it was time for her to leave, I walked her out to the front door. As we said goodbye, she paused for a while, like she didn't really want to leave. I took my chance to ask her what was going on.

"Sue, are you okay?" I asked gently. "You seem to be really distracted. I know you've had a lot going on, but is there something else you'd like to tell me?"

Sue shifted her weight back and forth, wringing her mittened hands together. I took her momentary silence to mean that there was something else going on. It was like she was deciding if she really wanted to divulge the information to me.

"I'm just a bit distracted," she finally said. "But there isn't much I can tell you about."

"I'm always here if you need to talk," I said. Sue may not have a family, but we were the closest thing she did have.

"Thank you Tessa," she said.

As I watched her leave from the front window, I thought about Rich again. Maybe I should have asked her specifically about him. But she already seemed so sad. I didn't want to make it even worse. Besides, we didn't have time to dwell on Rich right now. We had another grand opening to plan out.

•Chapter Sixteen•

The beginning of the week had flown by in a bustle. I had been able to have the local paper put in a story about the new grand opening. I had also been able to have a different reporter do the story, so the story was actually about the store and not the murder. I worked on the window displays in the evening, spending the days working at the B&B and getting the outside decorated for the contest while also making sure my mother was well taken care of.

Finally Wednesday dawned and it was such a big deal in my family that we helped my mother get ready and bundle up before getting her in the station wagon along with a wheelchair we rented for the occasion. When I had told her about our plans for the grand opening, she had told me that in no uncertain terms would she miss it.

That morning, we had put up the ribbon in front of the door to drum up some more interest. The longer the ribbon was up, the more people would see it and remember our ribbon cutting ceremony that night. Between that and the deal that Sue had decided to offer on most of the Christmas ornaments, we were hoping for a stellar night.

Now a crowd was starting to gather outside of the door as Sue and I waited inside. Rich's daughter

Marie had come over with a giant pair of scissors that Rich had been planning to give Sue for the ceremony. Marie had seemed cold and nonchalant, not wishing us a good opening. She probably didn't have room for good feelings right now as her father was in jail and she had to keep running the Loony Bin.

Outside, bundled up locals of all ages were gathered. Main Street had been shut down for the event so that people could walk up and down without being afraid of being hit by a car. Right now, they were all turned to face the high school choir who was standing in the middle of the street singing a few songs that they had thrown together last minute for us. When I had approached the choir director, it turns out Sue had just brought her a hot dish for supper a month or so ago when her kids were sick at home. She agreed to put on a good performance for the opening and she had delivered.

Inside, I was starting to get nervous. What if the only people who came were looky-loos? What if they didn't actually want to come inside or they came in, but only to see where a murder had occurred instead of buying anything? I just wanted this to be as successful as possible for Sue.

We could just barely hear the choir outside as they finished up their last song. The crowd applauded and then shuffled around to face the store again. I turned to look at Sue.

"Let's get out there and get this ribbon cut," I said.

I grabbed the giant pair of scissors and opened the door for Sue to go through first. It was her store, so it was only right for her to go first.

My dad and Tank were standing just to the right of the door with my mother in front of them in her wheelchair. She looked the coziest of all, all wrapped up in a fluffy blanket. Mandy and Trevor were next to them and I could see Clark standing at the back of the crowd. I smiled at my family and gave a little wave to Clark, who winked at me over the heads of some of the townspeople. Max was on duty, so I had figured I wouldn't see him at the grand opening and I was right.

"Welcome everyone," I said once the talking had died down a bit. "We are so glad you are here to help us open this shop. I personally have seen how exciting this entire idea has been for Sue and I have been so glad to help her with this passion project of hers. Now, I'll turn it over to the woman of the hour."

Everyone clapped for Sue as she shyly smiled. The sparkle in her eyes had returned a bit and I was glad to see she had perked up.

"Thank you everyone," she said quietly. "I hope you all love this shop as much as I do. I have picked out every item in here and I hope you love them. Without further ado, I'm going to cut the ribbon."

104

I handed her the giant pair of scissors and after she tried to wrangle them all by herself with little success, I helped her pick them up and clip the ribbon. As it fell to the ground, the crowd clapped and cheered again and a few camera flashbulbs went off.

Sue was the first person back into the store followed by Tank, who had agreed to come in right away to help with the initial surge of customers. I stepped back and pressed myself against the wall. I couldn't move anywhere else as the people pushed into the store. My parents hung back, not wanting to try to maneuver a wheelchair through the giant, bustling crowd. I gave them a little wave as I waited to be able to cross over to them.

First, though, I saw Jill coming through the crowd. She was only wearing a thin fleece jacket and she looked upset, but I wasn't sure why. She may just be too cold. I put my hand out and grabbed her arm as she came by me.

"Oh hi there Tessa," she said, stepping over to stand next to her. "You did a great job of getting the store back on it's feet."

"Thanks Jill," I said. "How have you been? I hope you haven't had to be out of your apartment too much for the police."

"Oh no," Jill said, her eyes darting around. "They did come up and do a quick interview with me, but otherwise I haven't really been bothered by them. I've been busy making a lot of jewelry for the store, do you think I could bring them in tomorrow? I didn't want to bother you too much before the grand opening."

I nodded and studied her face. Jill's eyes were puffy and red. She looked like she hadn't been sleeping well, like she had been up all night crying instead. I didn't know Jill very well but I just couldn't stop my mouth from shooting off.

"Are you okay Jill? You look like you've been crying."

Jill's cheeks went red and she reached up to touch her face. Now, she just looked embarrassed instead of upset. That is definitely not the reaction I had wanted from her.

"Oh yeah," she said. "I was just watching a sad movie while I finished up a few more necklaces to sell. I should probably just go back up to my apartment if I look that bad."

"You don't look bad," I said in a hurry. "I just wanted to make sure you were alright."

"That's really sweet of you," she said. "Have a good evening."

Jill turned and rushed away so quickly that she bumped into an old lady who was trying to come into the store, causing her to stumble. As someone in the crowd grabbed the lady to make sure she didn't fall down, Jill continued on without even offering an apology.

As I waited for the crowd to finally die down, I thought about how weird that interaction had been. I didn't really know Jill, so maybe she was just an anxious person in general. I decided not to hold it against her. It had been a weird week for all of us.

Instead, I walked up and down Main Street with my parents as we waited for the crowd inside the Christmas Shop to die down a bit and make enough room for a wheelchair to come in. We bought a corndog from a food truck for dinner and a funnel cake for dessert. Then we sat on a picnic bench that had been set up as we listened to holiday music that was being piped out over some speakers.

This was the first year that Shady Lake had put on this holiday shopping event and from what I could see, it was a raging success. The streets and shop were filled with people and the entire area was so festive that it looked like it should be a picture in a calendar.

The tops of the buildings were lined with large, white lightbulbs and garlands with lights were strung from lamppost to lamppost and crisscrossed across the street. Large wreaths were hung on every lamppost and a large Christmas tree had been erected in the small park at the end of the street. The tree lighting ceremony had happened on Black Friday, but unfortunately we had missed it because of the murder and then Tank being questioned. I promised myself I would go next year. At least I was seeing it now.

The town Christmas tree was a real tree that had been planted in the park decades ago and was decorated each year with strands of large Christmas lights and big, plastic ornaments. There was a giant gold star on the top which had been put on shortly before the tree lighting ceremony last week. It also had a light inside, so even when it was dark you could see the star shape at the top. It was extraordinary to look at and I almost couldn't tear myself away, but I knew my mother was dying to see the Christmas Shop.

When we got back to the store, the initial rush had cleared out and while there were still a lot of people browsing, it was clear enough to bring a wheelchair through. I helped lift the chair up over the lip of the front door and my parents went off to browse while I went to see how Sue and Tank were doing. Tank was running the register while Sue flitted around the store helping customers. It looked like her spark was back, at least for now.

I waited while Tank rang up a few purchases and the next time he hit a small lull in people wanting to pay, I stepped up to the counter. I had to smile at the uniform that Sue had decided on. It was just a red shirt with a little green apron over it and a red Santa hat. It was easy, but also festive.

"How is it going?" I asked. I had snuck a peek at his cash register's drawer during the last few transactions and it looked pretty full of cash which made me extra happy.

"Really good," Tank said with a toothy smile. "We've had a steady stream of paying customers ever since you guys cut the ribbon. And people are buying lots of things, not just the cheap stuff."

"I'm so glad to hear that," I said. I lowered my voice to a whisper. "I was a little bit afraid that people would just come in to look at where it happened."

"You weren't the only one who was afraid of it," Tank said. "Quite a few people have also mentioned that to me. But it really is going great. Hopefully we can keep up the crowds."

I was going to keep talking, but just then another customer came up with purchases to pay for. So I waved goodbye at Tank and went to find my parents. They were standing next to the giant nativity set I had set up, admiring the craftsmanship. I was happy to see that most of the boxed pieces had already sold.

"We were just waiting to say goodbye," my dad said as I walked up.

"And we were admiring this beautiful nativity set," my mother said.

"Isn't that great?" I said. "It is all hand-crafted. And would you like me to drive you home? I'm not

109

ready to leave, but I can drive you home and come back."

"Oh, I don't think you'll have trouble finding a ride home," my mom said, nodding behind me.

I turned and saw Clark standing next to the Christmas tree by the door. When I caught his eye, he gave me a little wave and started to walk towards me. I turned back to my parents and blushed a bit, but said my goodbyes.

"Hi there, would you like to go walk around a bit?" Clark asked.

"Sure, as long as you can provide a lift home later," I said, smiling at him.

"I think I can do that," he said as he slipped his hand into mine. I waved one more time at my parents before Clark and I left to walk up and down Main Street, taking in the holiday magic together.

•Chapter Seventeen•

My mom's vision for the holiday decorating contest had been intricate and detailed. Thankfully I had roped Clark into helping. Once school was over, he had driven straight to my house in his old pickup truck and then I had put him to work.

The theme of the B&B was backyard birds, so my mother had envisioned larger than life displays of the different birds. Thankfully, I was semi-artistic and had painted some large pieces of plywood as large blue jays, cardinals, and chickadees. Then I had taken blue, red, and white Christmas lights and outlined each bird in the appropriate color.

Now, Clark was helping me figure out how to get them set up in the yard. We needed them to be firmly set up so that wind or heavy snow couldn't knock them over, but we needed to make sure it didn't look too cheap either. While he did that, I worked on the other part of the plan.

We had a little backyard shed that we had dragged into the front yard. We lined it with Christmas lights and put up a Christmas tree outside of it. We wanted it to look like the birds were decorating for Christmas. The problem right now was that we didn't want it to be too cartoonlike. Of course, I wasn't sure how to tell my mom that there really wasn't a way to make "birds decorating for Christmas" look elegant and classy.

I stood on the sidewalk in front of the B&B looking at the display and wondering what we could add or change. Clark was busy getting the birds stood up which was honestly helping quite a bit. I had been hard at work all day on this display and I needed a distraction now.

I scooped up a handful of snow in my mittens and shaped it into a ball. Clark was busy attaching some poles to the back of one of the cardinals, so I snuck up behind him and yelled his name. When he straightened up and turned to look at me, I chucked the snowball straight at him, hitting him square in the chest.

"Tessa!" he shouted in surprise. He scooped up a bunch of snow and I was not going to take any chances. I turned and hightailed it into the backyard.

I hid behind a bush and quickly made another snowball so that when he came running around the corner of the house I nailed him with an other snowball, this time right in his stomach. I had made the mistake of blocking myself in so that once I started running, he already had a head start and easily caught up to me to hit me in the back with his snowball.

Clark grabbed me around the waist and tackled me into a snowbank. He pretended like he

112

was going to push my face in the snow and whitewash me, but instead he just leaned down and gave me a big kiss. We laid for a little while in the snow, kissing and holding hands. We were both dressed for the weather, so laying in the snow was okay, especially when we were warming each other up.

"Hopefully next time you'll think twice before you try to start a snowball fight with me," Clark said with a laugh. "I let you off easy this time."

"I'll remember that next time," I said. "I just really needed a break from the work and you were an easy target."

Clark laughed and stood up, offering me his hands to help me stand up. Still holding hands, we walked back to the front yard. Before I had nailed him with a snowball, Clark had finished up getting the last bird in the ground. The scene was coming along nicely which was good considering the judging was tomorrow.

"Let's take a picture and then go in to show my mom how it is going," I said. "After all, it is her design and she should get final say in what we do."

Clark nodded and looked back and forth before walking into the middle of the street to get a picture of the entire house and yard. He knew the drill. My flip phone had a camera, but it was a terrible one. So he knew that I would need to use his smart phone camera for the picture.

Once back inside, we shed our outside clothes and made ourselves two giant mugs of hot chocolate with marshmallows before heading upstairs to see what my mother thought of the display.

We found her in her regular spot in the living room. She was on the couch with an ottoman in front of her, her cast propped up on top of it. She had a TV tray next to her that held the television remote, a water bottle, a bottle of pain relievers in case her leg started to ache, and a puzzle book with a few pencils. Her crutches were leaning against the arm of the couch, ready for the next time she needed them. We usually weren't too far away from her, but we did want to make sure she was okay in case we were busy.

I sat down next to her on the couch and Clark sat on the chair. He handed me his phone and I pulled up the photo he had taken of the front of the house to show my mother. She zoomed in and studied it carefully, slowly moving over the entire scene to take in all of the parts. After a while, she handed the phone back to Clark.

"That's coming along nicely," she said. "I do think it could use some more razzle dazzle if we are going to win the contest though."

I tried not to look too disappointed. I had been hoping she would say it was done because I still had a lot of things to do and I was hoping to cross this one off of my list. I still had to finish buying presents for the entire family, not only from me but from my parents also. That was one thing I could not entrust to my father because he couldn't follow a shopping list if his life depended on it. Last time we sent him to the grocery store with a very specific shopping list, he had come back with none of the items on the actual list, but he did buy a sheet cake decorated with a pirate ship and the biggest jar of pickles I had ever seen.

My father had been tasked with wrapping the gifts we did have so far because he was really good at wrapping. He would wrap the rest of them, as soon as I had bought them all. He would also be tasked with planning and doing a lot of the actual cooking for Christmas, but obviously I would have to go shopping for all of the supplies first.

"What else can we do Mom?" I asked. I was tired of coming up with the ideas. I figured if she had an idea of what we could do, I could implement it. But I was too tired to do the thinking right now. I was just glad the investigation was over so that I didn't have to think about that, even if I had a vague feeling that Rich hadn't done it.

"Let me think for a moment," my mother said. "I have an idea, but I need to think for a second before I try to tell you what to do."

Clark and I sat sipping our hot chocolates as my mother closed her eyes, losing herself deep in thought. Clark winked at me over his mug and I felt myself start to blush. Thirty years old and I still lost my cool when it came to my love life and my parents. I could see why Tank wanted to keep his maybe girlfriend a secret.

"Okay, I've got it," my mother said, her eyes popping open. She pushed her self up to situate herself better. "So far we have some birds decorating for Christmas, right? Well I think we need to add a North Pole scene."

I sat for a moment, hoping she was kidding. I'm not sure how the North Pole was connected to backyard birds other than they both had to do with Christmas.

"I'm thinking you whip up a few more plywood decorations of Santa and Mrs. Claus with a few elves," she said, apparently unaware that I didn't just 'whip them up' because they took actual time to get done. "I think the shed looks nice, but let's turn it into Santa's workshop so that the birds are actually decorating Santa's backyard."

As she explained in way too much detail exactly what needed to be done to the display, I had to admit it was a good idea and if I could get it done in time, it just might win us the contest. The trouble would be just getting everything done before Santa

116

came down the chimney.

•Chapter Eighteen•

I had only gotten three hours of sleep the past night, but I had carried out my mother's vision. The plywood backyard birds were now officially decorating the backyard of Santa's workshop. My mother had put her stamp of approval on it and now we just had to wait for dusk so the judges could go around and see all of the holiday decorations.

Clark had even come over early before he headed to work to help me get them set up in the yard. I wasn't sure what he saw in me, but I was so grateful for him. Not only was he handsome, but he came over to help me with crazy things like decorating the yard. That was a man worth keeping around.

Now I was sitting in the living room trying not to fall asleep while I took a few minutes to regroup. With everything that had been going on, there hadn't been much time to sit and relax. I had a piece of paper where I was making a to do list for myself. It was only the beginning of December, but I still wasn't sure I'd be able to get everything done before Christmas.

There was a soft knock on the door and I went to open it. We weren't expecting any new guests today and I don't think anyone had ordered anything to be delivered, so I wasn't sure what to expect. When

I opened the front door I was surprised to see Jill standing there.

"Hi Tessa," she said with a smile. "I know you weren't expecting me, but is there any way I could come inside and talk to you?"

"Umm sure," I said. I was pretty confused because Jill and I weren't friends and honestly, we were hardly acquaintances. I had no idea what she could be here for.

I let her in and after she took off her boots and winter jacket, I had her follow me to the living room. We sat down on opposite ends of the couch facing the large front window where all of the bird feeders hung. For a few moments we sat in silence watching the various birds eating at the feeder.

"I'm sorry," I said. "You must think I have no manners. Would you like something to drink? We always have coffee, otherwise there is water or..."

"Oh no," she said, cutting me off before I could list the endless beverages we had. "It is me that doesn't have the manners because I came to ask you something that could come across as quite rude, so I hope you won't think badly of me."

I wasn't sure how to respond, so I just smiled at her. I hadn't heard the question yet, so I couldn't really tell her whether I thought she was rude or not. I mean, my big mouth and my passive aggressive Minnesotan nature would do battle over what to say to her if it was actually a rude question.

"I'm going to be really honest with you," Jill said. "The murder and investigation really threw me for a loop. What if the intruder had come up to my apartment? Anyway, I called in sick to my table waiting shifts for a few days because I just wasn't sure I could handle it and not I'm not sure I'll be able to pay my rent, not that I know who to pay anymore anyways."

I tried to not let my confusion show on my face. Was she asking me for money? I didn't even really know her.

"What I'm here for is that I know you've admired my jewelry in the past, so I was hoping that maybe you were still in the market for Christmas presents and that I could sell you a few pieces. We could both benefit from it."

Well that made a little more sense, I thought to myself. I had definitely spent time admiring her necklaces and I did need presents for my sisters.

"Okay, show me what you have," I said. "Why don't I run upstairs and grab my wallet while you take a few pieces out."

"Sure, sure," Jill said. "Take your time."

I took the stairs two at a time and ran to my room. I typically don't carry cash, but I did have a checkbook I could grab. I had found it in case I needed it to pay for the pizza the other night, so I knew exactly where it was. I grabbed it and headed back downstairs.

As I shut the door that separated our family area from the public area of the bed and breakfast, I was surprised to see Jill standing at the top of the stairs, just outside of the bedroom that was still blocked off with police tape. I couldn't tell if she had been reaching for the doorknob or if she had just been moving in a way that made it look weird.

"Oh, I was just coming to find you," she stuttered as she stumbled backwards a bit. "I just remembered that the pieces I grabbed to show you were actually ones I had promised to someone else. I'm sorry, I've been in a tizzy lately and now I've come all this way for nothing."

"Well not for nothing," I said. "I would still like to buy some jewelry from you for my sisters. Maybe we could meet another time?"

"Oh yeah," she said. "Let me give you my card and you can message me with some ideas for colors or styles so I can be a bit more prepared next time."

I took her card and shoved it into my checkbook. She stood there awkwardly looking towards the door of the closed off bedroom.

"Was that where Claire stayed?" she asked, pointing towards it.

"Yeah, it was," I said. "I actually need to talk to the police about it because we can't just have one whole bedroom shut off. If their investigation is over, they need to come free up this bedroom."

"Did they say the investigation is over?" Jill asked wide-eyed.

"Well, I don't think it's really over," I said. "But they have Rich in custody and from what I hear, an arrest is imminent. So I'd say the investigation is pretty much over."

Jill nodded exaggeratedly, like she was a bobblehead doll. I had heard that the murder happening just downstairs from her apartment had really affected her and now I was seeing evidence of that. I could understand being freaked out, knowing that someone had been killed and that it could have very possibly been you.

"Why don't you head back home and I'll let you know when I put a little more thought into the necklaces," I said. I put my hand on her shoulder and turned her around as I started to escort her down the stairs, but she stopped short at the top of the staircase.

"I did have one more thing," she said. "Before she died, I ran into Claire and she said she wanted to buy a necklace from me. I thought it was really weird, but I did give one to her to look at. She promised to pay me later and so I let her keep it because I didn't want to make her angry so that she would kick me out. Plus, I figured maybe I could get her to carry some in the dog grooming salon which seems really stupid now, but made sense at the time."

Jill was waving her hands frantically in front of herself as she talked and I could see that she was really upset. I put my hand on her arm to try and help her calm down a bit by grounding her. But her eyes were darting around as she talked.

"But if you find it," she was saying, "could you give it back to me please? It may seem insignificant, but I do have to pay for the supplies for each of my necklaces and every little bit counts for me right now."

"Sure I can," I said. "But I think maybe you should stay a little longer before you go home. Would you like a drink or maybe a piece of pie? We also have a little bit more Thanksgiving leftovers if you are really hungry."

Jill shook her head decisively back and forth. She walked down the stairs quickly and I hurried to catch up.

"No, I really should be going," she said. "But thank you for your offer. It is really sweet of you Tessa."

She grabbed her jacket off of the hook and jammed her feet into her snowboots before hurrying out the door without even putting her jacket on. I watched through the front window to make sure she was alright and she seemed to be as she backed out and drove back towards downtown. I wondered briefly if I should call the emergency line or maybe the non-emergency police number, but what was I going to tell them?

"Uh hi, a woman I barely know was acting weird. But maybe not because I don't really know so maybe she just always acts like that."

I decided I would go to visit her tomorrow and maybe bring some donuts. I had been so busy lately that I hadn't even had time to go to the Donut Hut for some donuts. I knew that was a good thing, but it didn't make me like donuts any less.

I glanced at my phone and saw that I only had a few more hours before the judging would begin. I decided I would work on some of the interior decorating until then, since that had been put on the back burner while we set up for the contest.

Down in the basement, there were dozens of cardboard boxes and big plastic tubs stuffed full to the brim with Christmas decorations of all sorts: ornaments, garlands, knick knacks and more. I really had my work cut out for me. I rolled up my sleeves and got to work.

•Chapter Nineteen•

By the time my family was all together and gathering by the front window to wait for the judges, I had accomplished a few majors details for the holiday decorating inside: the main staircase was now lined with a large, fake greenery garland that wrapped up the handrail. I could only assume by the size and how nicely my mother had packed it up that it had probably cost a fortune. There were also a handful of red, velvet bows beneath it that I had to space evenly on each side all of the way up. Let me tell you, symmetry is not my strong suit. It took me an hour just to get the bows right.

I had also put up a Christmas tree in the living room between the big bird-watching window and the fireplace. It was decorated with red and gold glass ornaments and a thin gold tinsel garland that wraps from the bottom to the star on top.

It turned out beautifully, but I also never wanted to decorate a "pretty tree" ever again. I much preferred the tree we put up and decorated in the family area. That one was an old fake tree that we had owned for over a decade. The needles were falling off and every year, it leaned a bit more to the left. We decorated it with all of the ornaments we had ever made or been given and they remained on the tree until we moved out.

My box of ornaments was one of the only things I brought back home with me after Peter died. Mostly because to me, home was where I kept my childhood ballerina ornaments and the puffy painted ornaments and movie tie-in ornaments we got from a fast food restaurant.

That tree wouldn't be put up until tomorrow, hopefully. And we always got help with that one. Even my siblings who had moved out of the house came home and helped decorate it. I had already told myself that when that happened, I was going to sit on my behind and simply direct.

Right now, we were all gathered at the window. My mother was front and center in her wheelchair, excitedly looking out for the official judge car to come around. She was almost like a little kid waiting for Santa she was so excited. My father was standing proudly next to her, his hand never leaving her shoulder. Occasionally she would turn and smile up at him and he would beam back at her. My parents are the reason I believe in true love and they are what I look to when I think about possibly falling in love again. I need that kind of love in my life, but not quite yet.

My siblings were milling around, mostly speaking to the few confused guests we had. Most of the guests we had were senior citizens who were visiting their grandkids, but didn't want to sleep over at their children's house but also wanted something a step above the local motel (which we also owned.) But once we mentioned the annual decorating contest, they understood the madhouse feeling around the bed and breakfast. It had been going on for a long time, just maybe not as big as it was now.

Clark was also there. I had invited him to come for the judging seeing as he had done a large share of the grunt work. He had brought over a large tray of meats, cheeses, and crackers which was a smart move because if there was one way to win over the Schmidt clan, it was bringing munchies to a family event.

Even Tank was there. Sue had told him he could have an hour off to see the judging before going back to the shop. He stood there in his green apron with a big goofy smile on his face, joking around with Teddy. I was glad to see him back to his old self, even if he did spend most of his time working at one place or another.

Suddenly, a pickup truck pulled up. It was lined with Christmas lights and in the back were a bunch of folding chairs with the judges sitting on them. If the judges hadn't been police, I'm sure this kind of rig would have been pulled over immediately. But the driver drove slow enough so that everyone remained in their seats with their official clipboards. It was dark, but as they got closer I could see Max sitting towards the back and I gave him a little wave from the window.

One of the most important rules to remember for the contest was that we were to remain in the house until the truck flashed its lights. Then we would know to come out and we could talk to the judges. Obviously it being a small town, the judges knew who lived in each house. But doing it this way meant it was somewhat fair because you couldn't describe or talk up your design.+698-

We waited nervously as we watched the judges get out and walk up and down the sidewalk in front of the B&B. The only sound was Tank continually snacking on the platter of food Clark had brought over because this was his dinner break and that meant he had to inhale enough food to get him through to his snack break.

Finally, the lights on the truck flashed and we all piled outside letting my mother, who was being carefully carried by Tank, Clark, and my father in her wheelchair, lead the way. Once they got to the sidewalk, the men put the chair down on the ground and my mother sat regally surrounded by her family.

"Hello Mrs. Schmidt," Max said as he stepped forward. "I understand this display was your idea. Could you tell us a little bit about it?"

My mother's smile lit up the dusky light and she nodded before folding her hands in her lap. The police judges gathered around her chair, some bending down to hear her better.

"Well our bed and breakfast here is bird themed, so I wanted to incorporate that into our display," my mother said. "But when that part was done, it just wasn't good enough. And then I had a thought: if birds were going to be decorating, wouldn't they be decorating at the North Pole too?"

She smiled for a moment before continuing. The judges were all nodding politely and I tried to read their expressions. Most of them were doing a pretty good poker face, which I assumed came with the territory of being a cop. A few seemed quite pleased, which made me hopeful that we would win a prize this year.

"I think this year our display has done a nice job of being something that can be enjoyed by all ages," my mother said as she gestured towards the display. "The kids will be delighted by Santa's Workshop while the adults will enjoy the inclusion of birds we see every day here in Minnesota. I hope you enjoy it as much as I do and if you have any questions, please feel free to ask."

The judges all looked at each other to see if anyone had a question, but after a few shakes of the head, it was apparent that my mother had said all they needed to hear. My siblings and broke out in raucous applause while a few of the judges offered a polite clap.

After some thank yous and a few handshakes, the judges climbed back up into the back of the truck so they could continue on to the next display they needed to judge. I gave Max another shy wave as they started rolling and he winked back at me.

We all rushed back inside to the living room where we had pulled out and plugged in the giant, old radio we kept mostly for emergencies. The winners of the decorating contest would be announced on Shady Lake's radio station, WARG. It was the only way that made sense because television programming couldn't be preempted for the announcement and no one wanted to go gather in the cold just to find out they potentially didn't place. So everyone tuned in and once the police made their decision, they drove to the radio station and announced it live on air.

While we all waited, the station was playing Christmas carols broken up every once in a while by the announcer coming on to say that the police were still not there to give the announcement even though that was what we were all waiting for.

As we picked at the snack tray and Tank kept checking his watch to make sure he wasn't going to be late to help Sue close up the Christmas Shop, we sipped the batch of hot cider we had whipped up. It warmed us back up after being outside with the judges and gave us something else to nervously fiddle with.

Finally, after an old rock and roll Christmas song, the announcer came back on the air.

"Well folks, the police have just walked into the studio here, so I'm going to turn it over to them," the announcer said. "So without further ado, here is the moment we've all been waiting for."

There were some sounds of someone at the radio station fiddling with the microphone. Then Max's voice came booming over the air. I smiled at the sound of the familiar voice.

"Hello there everyone," he said. "I'm Officer Max Marcus and I've been given the wonderful job of announcing the winners of this year's contest. First, I'd like to say that we saw so many wonderful lights displays this year and it is always hard to pick the winners. So I'd like to congratulate everyone for their wonderful displays and the hard work they put into them."

Clark sighed behind me. He and Max got along fine, but obviously they weren't really friends since I was casually dating both of them. Sometimes Clark got a little tired of Max's local yokel, good boy personality, which was exactly what I liked about Max. I shot him a look and he gave me a guilty smile back.

"So in third place is the Santa's Workshop

Backyard scene put up by the Shady Lake B&B," Max announced.

The living room erupted in cheers. We were hoping for first place of course, but any place was worth celebrating since we'd never been able to crack the top three. My father gave my mother a big hug and Tank picked me up and squeezed me so hard that I could hardly breath.

After much celebrating, Tank said a goodbye and ran out the door to deliver the good news to Sue who probably had already been listening at the shop. The rest of us decided that we needed to order some pizza from Mike's to celebrate.

As we sat around eating the cheesy, greasy slices of pizza, I didn't feel guilty for once. It had been a lot of hard work to get that display up and while I still had a lot things to do before the holiday season was over, at least the decorating contest was over and the police had settled on their murder suspect.

•Chapter Twenty•

The morning after the decorating contest, I met Sue outside of the Christmas Shop to help her open up. This time though we didn't walk into the scene of a crime. It was Saturday, so I had volunteered to help her on what promised to be a busy day. Of course, that had been before my mother had broken her leg. Thankfully my sister Trina was done with finals and agreed to stay the night so she could look after the B&B desk and my mother. With some juggling, I got all of my bases covered.

After we got all of the lights on in the store and made sure the shelves were straightened, I volunteered to run and grab us some coffee and donuts. It was a mild November morning, cold enough for the snow to stay while not so cold to take away my breath while I walked. It was cloudy and gray, but all of the Christmas lights downtown were lit so it wasn't a gloomy sort of morning.

I pushed open the front door of the Donut Hut and waved hello to the regulars while I made my way to the counter where Mandy was standing. When she spotted me, she gave me a big grin.

"I haven't seen you here recently," she said teasingly.

"Yeah, my waistline needed a break," I said

133

while she gave a laugh. She knew my weakness for sweets. "But I can't stick around. I'm working at the Christmas Shop this morning and I came for some coffee and donuts for Sue and I. Can you get that packed up?"

"Of course, coming right up," she said. I watched her pack a cardboard box with four seasonal donuts and two big to-go cups with coffee. That was exactly what I needed for this cold, cloudy morning. I gave her a big thank you and left, waving to Ronald and avoiding a glare from Chelsea along the way.

Once I was back at the Shop, Sue was just finishing up with a customer. The store was empty for now, so we sat down on the two stools she kept behind the register and ate our breakfasts. I silently cursed Mandy for giving me so many donuts as I reached for my second one. I promised myself that I was most definitely not going to eat a third.

"Tessa, I've been meaning to ask you how you've been doing since last week," Sue said. She started to ramble a bit while I tired to finish the bite in my mouth. "You know, since we found Claire. Have you been alright? I know you were trying to help Tank out, which it seems like you did."

"I've been okay," I said. "Of course it was upsetting to find her, but I've been able to get over it. And I had to help Tank. I just knew he didn't do it."

Sue picked at her donut and I noticed a glint of

gold on her wrist, but it was quickly covered by her sleeve. I tried to watch it while not looking too weird for staring at her arms. Could it possibly be a charm bracelet?

"And what do you think about Rich doing it?" she asked quietly. Her sleeve stayed just low enough that I couldn't see her arm. "Do you really think it was him?"

I took a bite of donut and then a drink of coffee. I thought about what I wanted to say, but first I really wanted to see what was on her arm. Then I spotted a tissue box on the shelf behind Sue's head.

"Could you please pass me a tissue?" I asked.

As she reached up for one, her sleeve fell down her arm revealing a bunch of bangle bracelets and right in the middle, a gold charm bracelet with charms similar to the one I had found on the floor next to Claire. I tried not to react. Was Sue asking me about what I thought of Rich because she was the killer and she wanted to make sure I didn't investigate any further? I blew my nose a few times to stall even more while I tried to figure out what to do.

"Well, I was pretty sure he didn't do it when the police initially brought him in, but now I'm not so sure," I said. "He was pretty angry when Claire came and from what I heard, they found some of his cigar ash here in the store. What do you think? You were pretty good friends with Rich weren't you?"

Sue looked around as if someone may have materialized in the store without us noticing. Of course, we were the only two in the place. The bell on the door would have definitely told us if someone else had come in.

"Rich and I have been friends for a long time," Sue said. "We've known each other since we were in school. I just don't think he would do it, but I don't know. Will you be investigating any more?"

"No, if the police are satisfied, then I am also," I said. Of course, I had enough on my plate and while I wasn't actually sure if Rich had done it, I needed to focus my attention elsewhere.

Sue looked unhappy for a moment, but quickly covered it up by taking another sip of her coffee. I wasn't sure how to read her face. I studied it over my coffee cup as I took another drink. Just then the bell over the door rang as another customer came in. Sue jumped up off of her stool and scurried over to greet them while I was left to clean up and puzzle over what had just happened.

I gathered up the garbage and went to throw it away in the warehouse where I could stand for a moment and collect my thoughts. I needed to think about what had just happened. The warehouse was a bit cold because it wasn't as insulated as the front of the store. I hugged my arms around myself as I ran through the conversation Sue and I had just had.

Sue had been wearing a gold charm bracelet with charms just like the horse one I had found on the floor. Had it come off as she struggled with Claire? Was Sue really the killer? She seemed awfully interested in the investigating I had done.

But of course she would be interested. The murder had happened in her store and now a friend of hers had become the main suspect. It made sense that she would ask some questions. Sue had seemed to be hinting that she didn't think Rich was the murderer. Was that because she was the killer or just because she had known Rich for so long?

I would need some more time to puzzle this all out and I would once I got home this afternoon. I made a quick decision to also do a bit of my own investigating in Claire's room. I know I had told Sue I was done with investigating, but now I wasn't so sure.

For now, I had to keep on with my work at the Christmas Shop. I headed back out front to see if Sue needed help. She was talking to someone who was looking for some specifically colored ornaments for their Christmas tree and there was another customer waiting at the counter.

I rushed over and started to ring up the woman's purchases. As I waited for her to rifle through her wallet to find the card she wanted to pay for her purchases with, I stole another glance at Sue.

She was smiling at the woman she was helping while they sorted through ornaments on one of the shelves. She looked like a happy, middle aged woman. Could she really be the killer?

I was snapped out of my thoughts by the customer I was helping waving her credit card under my nose a bit aggressively. I took it from the customer with a smile despite the woman's sneer and told myself I needed to just keep my head in the game. If Sue was the killer, I couldn't let her know I was on to her because that would just put me into even more trouble.

•Chapter Twenty-One•

Tank came in to the shop around noontime and we traded off. I drove back to the B&B to let Trina get back to her Christmas shopping. My mother had convinced my father to take her out to do some of their gift shopping as a way to thank me for all of my hard work on the outdoor display. Once I watched them drive off, I was all alone in the B&B. Now was my chance to do a little investigative work in Claire's room.

I tip-toed up the stairs, freezing as the stairs creaked under my feet. Even though I knew I was the only one there, it still made me nervous to be breaking into yet another police taped area. At least this one wasn't a murder scene. But I still really did not want to get caught in Claire's room. I took the key that I had grabbed from the front desk out of my pocket and unlocked the door, glancing around one more time before ducking under the police tape and shutting the door behind me. I used a tissue to avoid touching the door handle just in case the police would come back and re-dust it for prints or something.

The gloomy, cloudy day outside was making it somewhat dark in the room and I thought briefly about going out to grab a flashlight before I realized how foolish I was being. No one would notice if I turned the lights on because these rooms backed up to a mostly wooded area. Even if someone noticed, they would just think one of the guests had turned the light on. It was no reason for someone to call the police. So I flipped the switch by the door and looked around.

The police had been pretty considerate with their search. It wasn't what I would call neat, but it also wasn't like they had come in and thrown everything around either. When I thought of a police search, I imagined them rifling through drawers, throwing things all over the floor and dumping out suitcases onto the bed. Thinking about the police, I really needed to call them and ask if we could come in and clean up the room officially.

I pulled on a pair of winter gloves I had grabbed just in case the police did need to come back in. I didn't want to contaminate the scene with my fingerprints or DNA. The last thing I needed was to be even more involved than I already was.

I didn't really know what to look for. I knew I wanted to find the necklace for Jill, but otherwise I just figured I'd look around a bit to see what I could find. I started with Claire's personal things.

Her suitcase was open on the bed. I wondered if she had left it there or if the police had put it there. I shifted things a little, not wanting to move anything too much. I found a small jewelry bag and decided to look inside. There was a lot of jewelry inside, so I dumped it out on the night stand.

One thing that wasn't there was anything resembling a gold charm bracelet, which made sense considering that if the charm was from Claire's bracelet she would have been wearing it when she died. But judging from her other jewelry, a charm bracelet wouldn't fit with her style.

As I spread everything out, I found the necklace that Jill had been wanting me to find. It was a gold chain with a little green wire Christmas tree hanging from it. It was a beautiful piece, but as I picked it up, I noticed that it was broken. The Christmas tree fell off of the chain each time I tried to pick it up.

I left it on the nightstand and put the rest of the jewelry back into the bag which I replaced in the suitcase. Jill said Claire had taken the necklace and promised to pay later. But when had she done that? Had Jill been the last one to see Claire alive then? When I gave Jill the necklace back, I figured I'd ask her when that happened. I didn't think Claire had interacted with anyone more than for that five minutes, but I must have been wrong. Jill had been so shaken up that I hadn't wanted to ask her much of anything.

I decided to do one more sweep of the room to see if there was anything else missed by the police.

They typically did a pretty thorough job, so I tried to think of places they may forget to look. I looked under the bed and was somewhat pleased to see that there weren't even any dust bunnies underneath. We were doing a pretty thorough job cleaning then. Then I looked behind the TV stand. Nothing back there except the television wires.

Then it clicked with me. If they thought this was all cut and dry, they may have just looked through her things. The police may have ignored some of the elements of the room that were more standard for the bed and breakfast, like the decorations and such. I glanced at the pictures on the wall, but they all seemed to be in place. So did the little knick-knacks on the shelves and nightstands.

I looked at the small coffee table in the sitting room area of the bedroom. On the table was a stack of magazines and other things that may be of interest. Whenever the room was cleaned, the magazines were fanned nicely on the table. But when I looked at them now, they were in a stack.

Either the police had gotten in the habit of tidying up as they went or Claire had put them like that. Maybe there would be a clue inside. I crept over, still trying to be quiet despite the fact that I was the only person in the bed and breakfast.

I looked at each magazine carefully and picked them up one by one, shaking it by the binding to see if

142

there was anything hiding inside. Usually the magazines we left in the room were related to local things to do, bird watching, and interior decorating. But three magazines down the stack, I ran into a celebrity gossip, tabloid style magazine. One of these things is definitely not like the other.

•Chapter Twenty-Two•

As silly as it seemed, I held my breath for a moment, resisting the urge to sit down. I was fully aware that I may have been getting excited over nothing, but what if there was something in there? Something besides gossip about celebrity babies and cheating spouses.

I grasped the binding and shook it upside down once again but unlike the others, this time a piece of paper fluttered out. It landed on the floor, a piece of lined paper like the kind they used to write reports on in school. My heart was beating so hard that I was sure it would come right out of my chest. I tried to steady my breathing, but the butterflies in my stomach were making that hard to do. I stood and stared at the paper on the floor for a moment before I picked it up.

The paper was folded up into fourths and I could vaguely see the writing on the inside through the paper. I wondered what Claire was trying to hide. I didn't think she would go to the trouble of folding up her grocery list and hiding it in a celebrity magazine in a stack of other magazines.

I carefully started to unfold the note, taking care to not rip it or crease it in any way. Just as I got it open and saw that it was addressed to Claire, I heard the door to the garage slam downstairs.

"Tessa?" my father called. "Could you come here? I need some help getting your mother and all of the things inside."

I didn't want to shout to him from here, so I quickly took a plastic bag out of my pocket and shoved the paper inside. I hurriedly shut the door and locked it as quietly at I could. The bag and my gloves were put in my sweatshirt pocket so that I could look at the paper as soon as I got another chance.

Once I was at the top of the stairs, I called down to my dad to tell him I'd be right down. I took one more look at the door to make sure I hadn't disturbed the police tape, but it looked just the same as it had when I had come up the stairs earlier. No one would be any the wiser that someone had been in there.

I ran down the stairs, hardly noticing the creaking now that I wasn't sneaking around. My dad was standing the doorway to the garage, letting in a cold draft as he waited for me. I noticed that instead of bringing a load of things in as he came to get my help, he had come in empty handed. Sometimes he didn't think things through, but that was just how he thought.

"Hey Dad," I said. "Sorry, I was upstairs and I was washing my hands. I could hear you, but I didn't want to just scream down to you."

"That's alright Pumpkin," he said as he smiled at me. "I just need you to help me get your mom out of the car and bring in the stuff we brought. Of course we ended up with more than we went out for, but you know your mom."

We laughed together because we really did know my mom. She loved the holidays and everything about them. She loved to decorate, as evidenced by the extremely large outdoor display. My mom also loved to buy presents for everyone, usually way more than any of us needed. They would be wrapped up with large bows that doubled as accessories after they'd been torn off of the presents. Everything about her gift-giving was over the top.

I followed my dad out to the car and found that indeed the back of the car was stuffed full of shopping bags. My mother sat in the front, looking nonchalant as I gave her a look that told her she had gone overboard. She pushed open the car door and pretended she didn't see my disapproval.

"Tessa, as soon as I get inside, I have one more thing to ask of you," she said. "I had kind of forgotten about it with everything that has happened recently. But let's get me settled and then I'll go into details."

"Okay Mom," I said and I grabbed her crutches for her.

She managed to crutch her way to the stairs,

but once she got there she stopped and waited. My dad and I each took one side of her. She put her arms around our necks and we slowly, step by step helped her hop up the stairs. She took over at the top and used her crutches to get into the family room. She collapsed exhausted on the couch.

I had broken my leg as a kid and I remembered how tiring using crutches was. Now I tried to consider what it was like to use them as someone who was nearing retirement age. I figured it must be awful, which is why I tried to be of as much physical help as possible.

"I'll go back and get the bags," my dad said. "Some of the presents are for you after all and you can't see them before Christmas."

He turned and jigged back down the stairs and I turned to see my mother look like she was ready for a nap.

"I'll go make us some tea, okay?" I said. I figured it would give her a little time to potentially take a cat nap while I could hide the note so that I could read it later when I was all alone again. I was dying to open it now, but I didn't know how I'd explain it if anyone found me reading it.

My mother nodded with her eyes closed as I went to the kitchenette that we had in our family area. We ate the majority of our food downstairs using the real kitchen, but it was nice to have a little area to cook without having to venture into the rest of the bed and breakfast.

As the tea pot was heating up on the stove, I slipped over to my room and put the gloves and the plastic bag with the note into the drawer of my nightstand. Really, I could have put it just about anywhere because it wasn't like someone was going to come into my room looking for the note I had taken that no one knew about except me and a dead woman. But I felt a lot better knowing it was hidden away.

I put the tea bags in to steep and put some sugar and milk on a tray along with a few cookies. When I brought it all back into the family room, my mother was firmly asleep. I quietly set the tray down on the television tray next to her side of the couch.

She stirred as I sat on the other end of the couch and pretended like she hadn't been sleeping. When we were kids, my mother would always say that she was just resting her eyes and while I understood that phrase now that I was an adult, I also knew that she was totally cat napping each and every time.

"Oh good, I really need this," she said as she reached for one of the cups. "After shopping and being out in the cold with those stupid crutches, a hot cup of tea is just what the doctor ordered."

I grabbed the other cup and took a few sips.

Tea was definitely not my cup of tea. I would have taken a cup of coffee any day, but I had already been making a cup for my mother, so it had been easier to just make two. Besides, my mother razzed me about drinking too much coffee which was rich coming from someone who used to drink a steady stream of it from the time she woke up until she went to bed every day.

"Now, for what I wanted to talk to you about," she said. "I hope you don't have too much on your plate right now. I know that you are already so busy and having me out of commission has just added more stress. But I thought of one more holiday thing that I would love your help with."

I tried not to outwardly groan. It wasn't that I didn't like the holidays, but being so busy this year was enough to make anyone stressed and ready for Christmas to be over. Instead of grimacing, I took a Santa shaped cookie and bit off his head. I tried not to read too far into how I took out my stress and just tried to savor the sweetness as I nodded at my mom.

"Do you remember how I used to throw a holiday party every year?" she said.

Did I remember? Of course I did because it used to be one of the highlights of my year. Mom would pick a Saturday in December and invite literally everyone we knew. We all could invite any friends we wanted to. When party day came, the house would be bustling with people, practically bursting from Christmas cheer. Holiday carols would be pumping from the speakers and the entire first floor would be covered from wall to wall in Christmas lights. My memories from those parties included the special cookie decorating station for the kids, the hot chocolate that we would bring out to sit next to the fire pit in the back yard and dancing to some of my favorite carols.

"Well before I broke my leg, I wanted to start up my tradition of throwing a party again," she said. "So now I am wondering if you could help me with that. And before you say anything, I already picked the date and it is Saturday, so I'm not sure if that is feasible at all."

"Maybe we just cancel this year and try again next year," I said, hoping she would take me up on that.

"That had been my plan, but then today we ran into my friend Betty and she mentioned being excited to come to the party and I realized that I had already sent out one of those email invitation things to everyone in my address book, so we kind of can't cancel."

I let that hang in the air for a minute while I tried to wrap my head around everything I already had to do and adding planning a giant Christmas party to that. But how do I tell my mother no? She gave me life, she had welcomed me back into her home, and all she was asking was for me to throw together a party for all of our family and friends totally last minute.

"I know it is asking a lot," she said quietly before another sip of her tea.

"No, that's okay Mom," I said. I set my tea cup down. "I can do it. In fact, I have a few ideas to jazz it up. This just may be the best Christmas party we have ever thrown."

I collected our empty tea cups and brought the tray back to the kitchen. As I cleaned up our snack, I just hoped I could deliver what I had promised. The party was one thing I couldn't drop the ball on. I couldn't do that to my mother.

•Chapter Twenty-Three•

That night before bed, I waited until I heard my parents close their bedroom door before I took the note out of my nightstand to read. I didn't want anyone to accidentally burst in and see it, which was totally an unfounded fear because once all of my family members had passed the age of seven, they all become pros at knocking before opening a door. I felt kind of silly with all of the secrecy, but it felt like I had to be as secretive as possible.

I pulled the gloves back on my hands and opened up the little plastic bag. I pulled the note out and slowly opened it up. Once again, I saw that Claire's name was at the top in pen, but this time I scanned through the rest of the typewritten note. There wasn't much there to read which meant there wasn't much to try and figure out who wrote it

Claire,

Meet me at the Christmas Shop tonight around 10 so we can talk.

That was all it said. It wasn't even signed. I had gotten myself all worked up for nothing. In retrospect, I'm not sure what I thought it would say.

152

But I had hoped it would at least say who had written the letter.

I read it over and over again, but it was pretty cut and dry. There didn't seem to be any sort of hidden meaning or ways for me to tell who had sent it. I folded it up and put it back in the bag before taking off my gloves.

As I laid back on my pillows and looked at the ceiling, I wondered if I should turn in the note to the police. It probably wouldn't come to anything, but it seemed like something I should do. It technically was a clue in a murder investigation. But there was something about the note that still wasn't sitting right with me.

I got up out of bed and got ready to go to sleep. There was just something that was gnawing away at me. Something about that note wasn't sitting right. I brushed my teeth and put my pajamas on, but I just couldn't put my finger on it. Sleep came easily, which seemed about right because I spent all of my waking hours running around like a crazy chicken with my head cut off.

Suddenly, my eyes popped open and there was a thought in my head like I was just about to remember something. I glanced at the clock and saw that it was just past midnight. The moon was shining in my window and I laid as still as I could, willing the thought to come to me.

Suddenly, Max's voice echoed in my head.

"Our working theory is that Rich happened to see her going into the Christmas Shop to do some mischief as he was closing up the Loony Bin. We think that it made him so mad that he went in and the confrontation drove him into a fit of rage."

Claire had been invited by someone to meet at the Christmas Shop; she hadn't been there to do mischief. So who invited her? If Rich had, what would they have to talk about? I highly doubted Claire would have accepted an invitation from Rich, a man she had just met and only talked to for a few moments, to meet late at night at the Christmas Shop.

Besides, the only handwritten part of the note didn't look much like a man's handwriting. It was beautiful handwriting, almost too perfect. And while there were definitely males with nice handwriting, chances were that a woman had written that.

I sat straight up in bed. The only person who Claire would have been interested in meeting would have been Sue. She was the one that Claire needed to get out of the way. Claire probably went to the Christmas Shop hoping to get Sue to leave the Shop early. I would have to ask Sue if she wrote the note.

No, I couldn't do that. If I asked her and she had already killed, she could potentially kill again. That seemed like a ridiculous thought that little old Sue would go into a murderous rage, but laying by myself in the dark and watching the shadows dance on the wall could make anyone think dark thoughts.

Then an idea popped into my head. I could ask Jill. I needed to return that necklace to her anyway and she lived just upstairs from the Shop. Maybe she would know something, or at least be able to tell me if she had seen anyone's car that shouldn't have been there.

In the morning, I would ask her to meet. I would also let Max know about the note because if it proved Rich was innocent, I needed to make sure it found it's way into the right hands.

For now, I laid back down and shut my eyes. As hard as it would be, I needed to try and get more sleep, especially if I was going to be throwing together the party of the year and telling the police that they had the wrong guy in custody for the murder suspect I had stumbled upon.

•Chapter Twenty-Four•

Even though I am not a morning person, I was up with the birds the next morning. I just couldn't make myself sleep more after my middle of the night realization. I was even more excited about it because when I woke up in the morning, my realization still made sense, unlike other times I had middle of the night, mid-sleep cycle epiphanies.

I did wait nervously until a more acceptable hour when I could send messages to Max and Jill. I needed to speak with both of them about the murder and I had something to deliver to each one. First up was Max.

Hey Max, I have something really important to show you. Like 911 emergency important. When can we meet?

Then I sent a message to Jill.

Hey Jill, It's Tessa. I found that necklace you had been wanting from Claire's room. I also had a question for you. Let me know when I can come by and drop it off.

After waiting nervously for five minutes for either of them to answer and getting nothing in response, I decided a trip to the Donut Hut was in store. I needed to talk to someone and if Jill and Max weren't going to get back to me, I needed to talk to Mandy.

156

On my way down the steps, I happened to run into Trina, who was coming up to visit with our parents. I figured she may have been on desk duty when Claire got that note, so I asked if she had seen if anyone had brought something over for Claire that day.

"When I checked the mail that day, there was an envelope with Claire's name on it," Trina said. "It had been hand-delivered to the mailbox, so I have no idea who it came from."

I thanked her and continued down the stairs. Of course she hadn't seen who delivered it because that would make my life way too easy.

A short time later, I was sitting in a booth in the Donut Hut with a maple long john that had snowflake shaped sprinkles on top and a mug of coffee. Mandy was sitting across from me. Sunday mornings were feast or famine when it came to customers at the Donut Shop. There would be an initial rush when people woke up and then everything would slow while people went to church and then it would pick up again when families would come for after church donuts.

I was glad to come during a slow time when I could get not only my tasty breakfast, but also some time with Mandy. I didn't even have to whisper because most of the time while I was there, the only customers were people running in to buy a half dozen donuts to go.

After I finished telling Mandy about the note and my revelation, I sat back and took a large bite of my donut. Mandy seemed shell-shocked, like she couldn't quite believe what I just said. For a moment, I thought she was going to say something, but then she grabbed her coffee mug and took a drink. Finally, I just had to break the silence.

"So? What are you thinking?" I finally prodded. "Isn't that all just totally insane?"

"It definitely is," Mandy said. "But I think you might also be insane to think that Sue was the one who did it."

"I must admit, that is the one part of my new theory that I am not completely sold on," I said. "But who else would Claire have been wanting to meet?"

I took another bite of donut. Each time I bought another sweet, I promised myself that I would make a goal to stop eating so many sweets. I don't know when I would make that goal, but sometime I would. The new year would be here before I knew it.

"What if she just thought she was meeting Sue?" Mandy said. "Claire thought Sue wrote the note, so she went to the store. But someone else had written it and met her there instead."

"But who would do that?" I asked.

Mandy shrugged and I had to do the same. Really, any of the other suspects could have done it.

And we had only known Claire for such a short time. Maybe it was someone from out of town that had followed Claire to Shady Lake. Maybe the murder really had nothing to do with the Christmas Shop and it was purely coincidental that the murder had occurred there. If that was the case, how would we ever figure it out?

"Mandy, do you really think Rich did it?" I asked. "Like just look at the acts of the case. Does it make sense that he did it?"

"Yeah, I guess," she said. "Maybe he was worried about business with the dog grooming place next door so he got Claire to come just to talk to her but got so enraged that he killed her."

"Would you kill someone if they wanted to put a dog grooming place next door to the Donut Hut?" I asked her.

"No, but I think the fact that Claire was doing that and kicking a good friend of Rich's out of business to do that makes a big difference," Mandy said. "Overall, the whole situation would make me upset."

I nodded. Mandy was always able to put things into perspective for me. That was a nasty combination of circumstances and while I never condone murder, I do understand the anger that Rich may have had towards Claire.

"I am hoping Max will text me back soon," I

said. "I'm going to give him that note and see what he thinks."

"I think you have to," she said. Mandy checked her watch. "I need to get a move on. The after church rush will be starting any minute now. You want another cup of coffee to go?"

"You know I do," I said.

I grabbed the dishes and brought them back into the kitchen while she filled my travel mug with more coffee. I needed all of the coffee I could get because I was going to go tackle more of the inside decorating since we were now throwing a gigantic party in less than a week.

As I drove back home while sipping my coffee, I considered once again if maybe the murder's location was coincidental. I would bring that theory up to Max whenever he agreed to meet. As much as I understood what would make Rich so angry, I just didn't think he could kill over it.

•Chapter Twenty-Five•

Max had finally gotten back to me around lunchtime. He was a workaholic and it seemed like he was always on duty but when he wasn't working, he did like to sleep in. Police hours were so crazy that he often ended up losing sleep so that he could get things done.

Hey Sweet Thing, I'll come get you tonight and we can go get a drink. Is that 911 emergency soon enough?

I smiled when I read it. Max had been calling me Sweet Thing since we were in high school and it still made me blush with happiness every single time.

That'll be fine. See you later :)

The day was first spent dusting the main level and then hanging up holiday pictures and setting out holiday knick-knacks. Before my mother sprung this party on me, I had been planning on scrimping a bit on the interior decorations because I was just too busy to do everything. Thankfully, Trina was in town staying with her fiance over the holiday break and she was able to work the desk for me more than originally planned so that I had one thing I didn't have to worry about.

I lost myself so much in the decorating that I was confused to see Trina hurrying over to me as I was contemplating how to hang mistletoe in one of the doorways to the living room.

"You look like a mess," she said. "Isn't Max going to be picking you up in like two minutes?"

I pulled out my phone and flipped it open. Yikes! She was right.

"Thank you Trina," I said, jumping to my feet and running to the stairs. As I took them two by two, I called back over my shoulder: "If he gets here, please stall for me. I won't take long!"

I dashed past the living room yelling a hello to my mother before shutting myself in my room. Dating in a small town was not as easy as many might think. The nice thing about Max is that he is laid-back and doesn't expect me to spend hours getting ready. But anywhere we went out on the town, there would be someone there to judge.

Looking in the mirror, I saw a cobweb stuck to my hair on one side. Gross! I picked it out and ran a brush through it, glad that it was still relatively straight from when I had done my hair a few days ago. I swiped on some eyeliner and some lip gloss and then took a look at my outfit.

My outfit was currently an old t-shirt and jeans that were covered in dust. That obviously wouldn't do for a date. I pulled on a nicer pair of jeans and then looked in my closet. I had a drawer full of folded-up t-shirts in my nightstand, but I hung my nicer shirts in the closet. I tried not to take too much time on my decision, finally just pulling down a thin, sweater-like tunic that I put on over a tank top. I looked in the mirror and decided it would have to work for tonight.

As I pulled my bedroom door back open, I could hear Trina yelling up the stairs.

"Tessa, he is pulling into the driveway right now!"

"Thanks Trina. I'll be right down."

I grabbed my clutch purse and dashed into the living room to give my mother a quick hug before I bounded down the stairs. Max was standing just inside the front door and when he saw me, he smiled a wide smile. His blue eyes twinkled at me and I tried hard not to go to jelly inside.

"Let's go get a drink at the Loony Bin," he said, holding my jacket up so I could slip my arms in.

"Is that a good idea?" I asked, remembering how cold Rich's daughter Marie had been to us. "They aren't exactly going to be happy that you have their dad in custody for a murder."

"That's partially the point," Max said. He gave a quick wave to Trina and held the door open for me. He put out his arm to help me down the stairs and I gladly accepted, knowing my family wouldn't survive the holiday season if I slipped on the ice also.

"I want to show Rich's kids that there aren't any hard feelings on the side of the police," Max continued as he helped me into his car. He ran around the other side and hopped into the driver's seat. "And I wanted to tell you that he is no longer just a suspect. He is going to be put under arrest very soon."

Oh boy, Max was sure going to hate me when I showed him what the emergency had been about. He never liked it much when I messed up his investigations. I couldn't really blame him. I peeked inside my purse to make sure the little plastic bag with the note was still inside. It was in there between my flip phone and my wallet along with a miniature flashlight.

"That's actually what I wanted to talk to you about," I said. "See, I've done some looking around and I found something that I need to give you."

Max shot me a look. I put my hands up in defense, knowing a tirade about me not butting into his investigation was about to follow.

"Hear me out," I said quickly. "I went into the room Claire was staying in at the bed and breakfast because someone asked me to get something from in there. So I went in and I found something that may be relevant to your investigation."

"We looked all over that room," Max said as he pulled into a parking spot in the lot across from the Loony Bin and the Christmas Shop. He turned to look at me. "How would you have found something that we didn't find?"

164

"It helps when you work at the B&B and you can see when something is out of place, even if it is neat," I said. I explained the stack of magazines and finding the one that didn't belong and how the note fell out of it. I opened my purse and pulled out the little plastic bag with it inside.

Max tentatively took the baggie and looked at the note through the clear plastic. I told him what it said so that we didn't have to open it in the car.

"I thought it was important because I remember you saying that your theory about Rich being the murderer was that he found Claire in the store and confronted her," I said. "But this note proves that Claire was invited to the Christmas Shop by someone and I'm not a handwriting expert, but I think the handwritten bit was written by a female."

I left out the bit about Sue being the person that Claire probably wanted to meet and the fact that Sue wore a gold charm bracelet. The police would get to that point eventually and I wasn't even sure I was right.

Max sat for a moment staring at the bag before he looked up at me.

"You know, I'm always glad when your investigating turns up something useful," he said. "But you really know how to make my job quite a bit harder. We were just ready to arrest him and now we have new evidence to take into consideration."

"I know," I said. "But something was telling me Rich didn't murder Claire and I couldn't have him charged with murder when he wasn't the one who did it."

Max took my hand and gave it a squeeze. I held onto his large, familiar hand. Max's hands were always warm and seeing as it had started to snow outside again, they felt delightful.

"Here's what we are going to do," Max said. "I am going to have you put this back in your purse. Then we are going to go in there and have a drink. Then you are going to give me it again afterward and we are going to pretend we only did that once because then I'll have to immediately bring it in to the station. And I really don't want to cut our date short."

Max shut off the engine and hopped out of the car. After so many years of dating, I knew to sit and wait in the car until he went around and opened my door too. The first date we went on, I tried to get myself out of the car and he had been so broody that he finally got mad at me over our artichoke and spinach dip appetizer and told me that he always wanted to be the one to let me out of the car. We had actually laughed about that just a few weeks ago because while he did still like to open and close my door for me, he was no longer the angry, broody teenager we all seem to start adult life as.

As he opened the door and gave me his arm, I

smiled at him. Unlike with Clark, I didn't have to look up to Max because we were about the same height. I loved that about him because I could stare into his beautiful blue eyes much more easily. I looked into them now and knew I was the only woman he would break police policy for. I'm not sure he would have even done that for his first wife.

The rest of the night out went well. As expected, we received the stink eye from Rich's kids behind the bar, but it was somewhat off-set by Max throwing his hands up and telling them he came in peace. We had a drink and talked about the party I was suddenly planning.

"So don't be surprised if this is the last time you see me before the party," I teased. "I have so much to do that I don't even really know where to start."

"Well that's alright if I don't see you for a while," Max said with a wink. "Lately you've just been making more trouble for me."

I laughed before taking my last drink of wine. Max took the last dregs of his beer and stood up to grab our jackets. Ever the gentleman, he held mine up as I put my arms in. After throwing a few dollars onto the table for the server and waving to the regulars as we passed them by, we were out and back to the truck.

As Max drove me home, I grabbed his hand

and watched his face as we drove in and out of streetlights and the glow coming from the light displays. In high school, I was so sure I would be riding next to this man every day for the rest of my life. And then I left and we were over and I married Peter. But here I was, riding next to him again. Life was funny like that.

•Chapter Twenty-Six•

As someone who doesn't have a normal 9-5 job, Mondays usually aren't as terrible as everyone makes them out to be. But this Monday was definitely one for the books. I spent the day frantically cleaning the main floor of the bed and breakfast. At least the house was pretty clean to start with since people did stay here, but for a party I knew my mom had much higher standards. If some of these townswomen came and saw some dust in the house, they would gossip about it for quite a while and I didn't want that for my mother.

I have specific memories of coming home from school in the week before the party to see my mother cleaning literally every square inch of the house. She would pick a room, start at the top and clean everything: dusting all of the bits, cleaning ceiling fans, wiping down walls, cleaning baseboards, vacuuming furniture. If there was a way to clean something, it was cleaned.

I don't have a lot of patience when it comes to cleaning, but I did my best to make my mother proud. I started with the front entry and finished that and the dining room before lunchtime. I made a vegetable stir fry for my lunch and ate it in the living room with my mother. After all of the sweets and junk food, a simple vegetable filled lunch was just what the doctor ordered.

The next area to clean was the desk area, which I was glad about. I downloaded a true crime podcast on the desktop computer and listened to a story about a deranged doctor while I tidied. Of course we couldn't totally clear the desk area away as we were running a business, but I did put things in order and make a pile of things we needed for now, but that could be hidden away during the party.

"Knock knock," Mandy said. She knew not to actually knock, but came right in. She was holding two cups of coffee that she had brought in the extra, extra large travel cups she kept hidden away mostly for me. "I come with refreshment and an extra set of hands."

I rushed forward and grabbed the cup, slurping down the hot liquid. As much as I loved Mandy's donuts, I was extra happy to see she hadn't brought any with this time. I really wanted to be able to fit in my cute Christmas outfit but if I kept scarfing down the sweets I would need to wear my nightgown instead. I did give myself a pat on the back for my lovely, healthy lunch.

After a short break to drink a bit of coffee, Mandy and I headed to the kitchen to clean it top to bottom. The kitchen wouldn't really be seen during the party, but that is where all of the food preparation would take place and my mother had a rule that the cleaner the kitchen was before a large event, the easier it was to get the kitchen back to clean.

The cabinets were wiped down before we started on the counters. We worked in silence for a while, which is something you can comfortably do only with someone you've known for a long time. After a while, though, I needed to ask Mandy more about what she thought about Claire's murder.

"Mandy, you hear a lot of things at the Donut Hut," I said as I wiped off the containers of flour and sugar that we kept on the counter. "What have people been saying about the murder?"

"They mostly talk about how unfortunate it was for Sue," Mandy said. "It isn't like anyone really knew Claire, so they don't talk about her much except about her dog grooming plan. But no one is convinced that Sue or Rich really had anything to do with it. I think people have started to kind of forget about it, except for occasionally when they talk about how Rich shouldn't be the main suspect."

That made sense. I had met Claire, so I at least saw her as a person but for anyone who hadn't been in the Christmas Shop that day, she was more like a mythical creature who only came to Shady Lake to end up dead. But I understood that the concern was more for Sue and her livelihood.

"So I gave Max the note that I found

yesterday," I said. "I gave it to him right after he told me that they were going to formally arrest Rich."

Mandy had been down on her knees wiping off the lower cabinet faces, but now she sat back on her heels and stared up at me. She looked happily surprised by the news.

"Really? Good, I just can't imagine Rich doing it," she said.

"Don't worry, the note has thrown a wrench in that plan," I said. "But there is something else. I am starting to wonder if Sue really was the one who did it."

"Oh Tessa, really?" Mandy said. Her eyes were still wide with surprise, but this time it was a bit less happy. "Why do you say that?"

I told Mandy all about the charm bracelet I spotted on Sue's wrist and how it could potentially have been where the charm came from. Her mouth moved silently like she wanted to speak, but didn't know what to say. We went back to cleaning for a moment before Mandy finally spoke.

"Couldn't the charm have just fallen off Sue's bracelet while she was stocking the shelves or something?" she said. "Wouldn't that make the most sense?"

"If there hadn't been a murder that occurred right next to the charm, then I would agree," I said. "But haven't you noticed how weird Sue had been acting? She seems like she's residing in another dimension and just occasionally poking her head into ours to make sure everything is alright."

"I'm not sure how she is supposed to act after someone has been murdered in her shop," Mandy said. "I think I'd be in a tailspin for a while if someone died in the Donut Hut even if it wasn't a murder. What if someone was murdered here at the B&B? How would you feel then?"

She had a point. Death was hard and unexpected death was even harder. If it happened here, I know it would take a while to get back to where I felt okay. We continued to work in silence, moving on to scrubbing the oven and stove.

We silently got to a point where we agreed the kitchen was clean, so we plopped ourselves onto the chairs in the eating area of the kitchen so that we could finish our coffee.

"You know who else is acting weird?" I asked. "Jill. She asked me to find a necklace in Claire's room and I did, but when I messaged her to ask when we could meet, she hasn't gotten back to me."

"As someone who lives above her shop in downtown, I can tell you that I've had the worry that if someone broke into the Donut Hut, they would come upstairs after not finding much to take," Mandy said. "I understand being quite shaken that a murder happened basically in my home while I blissfully

173

slept upstairs."

Darn that Mandy and her empathy, always setting me right with my thinking. She was right though. A murder is going to make people connected to it act weird and it doesn't mean that they are the murderer.

Except in this case, one of them was the murderer and I wasn't sure it was the one they had in custody.

•Chapter Twenty-Seven•

When I woke up the next morning, I had a message from Jill saying she was free to meet that day. I had been starting to wonder if somehow she hadn't gotten my message, but I was glad she didn't wait much longer because as the party got closer, I had more and more to do. She invited me to come to her place late morning to return the necklace so after a bit more cleaning in the morning, I headed to Jill's house just before lunch.

I found the outer door that lead upstairs to Jill's apartment. While Sue's shop was definitely in an old building, it didn't look old from the shop. It was just cozy. But the stairwell and hallway up to Jill's door looked old and shabby. The floor was covered with a threadbare, blue carpeting and the walls looked dirty, but I wasn't sure if that was just the horrible lighting or if they were actually dirty.

Upstairs, there was only one door which I assumed was for Jill's apartment. I knocked on the door and waited. One of the lights started to flicker and I immediately stuck my hand in my purse and grabbed hold of my flashlight, just in case. But I didn't need to use it because just then, the apartment door flew open.

Jill was standing in the doorway, but she didn't

offer any sort of greeting. I tried not to read too much into her behavior because, as Mandy pointed out, she was probably still somewhat terrified. But unlike the other day, she didn't seem frantic today. She seemed almost devoid of emotion, like a strange robot.

"Hi Jill," I finally said. "Can I come in? I have the necklace for you."

Jill stared at me for another beat before plastering a smile on her face and stepping aside to let me in. As I came in, she shut the door behind me and I looked around. The apartment was small. I was standing in the kitchen and eating area right now and through a beautiful set of wooden columns, it was open to the small living room. There were two doors on the right side of the room and I assumed these were for the bedroom and the bathroom.

I followed Jill into the living room and saw that the windows looked over Main Street. They had a beautiful view of the holiday displays outside and I could imagine that the view of the lights at night was spectacular. The living room was sparsely decorated with a love seat and arm chair that didn't match, but seemed to be picked to complement each other. The couch was a green and dark blue plaid with a maroon throw on the back while the chair was mostly maroon with some dark blue buttons on the back.

Jill sat down on the edge of the seat and stared at me as I sat myself on the couch. I looked around and noticed how sparse the walls were. I remember moving somewhere and not hanging anything on the walls for a while because that just felt almost too adult and official. There were only two pictures, but they were set on the television stand. One was a family portrait and the other was of a horse.

I sat quietly while I took in everything around me. The quiet was making me a little nervous, but I wasn't sure why. The couch was scratchy when I put my hands down and for a moment, I almost forgot why I had come. But I knew Jill wasn't going to speak first, so I did.

"I found that necklace you were asking about," I said. I opened my purse and pulled out the little bag I had put it in. "I'm sorry, but it seems to be broken."

I handed Jill the bag which she took and stared at for a moment. She blinked a few times before she spoke.

"Thank you very much," she said. "I'm so glad you were able to get this back to me. It is very important to me."

"Really? Couldn't you just make another?"

"I can never make the same necklace twice," Jill said. When she looked at me her eyes were almost flashing, but I couldn't tell why. "Each necklace is infused with my thoughts and feelings at the time, especially necklaces like that one that are made for a specific person. It isn't just a bunch of wire I throw together."

I nodded and smiled at her. My parents had always taught me to never judge someone for their beliefs. I had done some reading about how ideas and feelings can hold some power, so as odd as it sounded I knew she wasn't actually too far off.

"Oh that's a lovely idea," I said brightly as I smiled at her. "Could I possibly bother you for a glass of water?"

"There's some water in the kitchen," Jill said, gesturing towards the small kitchen I had entered through. After waiting a minute for more instruction that didn't come, I stood up and made my way over.

As I opened and shut the cabinets to find a glass, I stole a glance through the opening between the rooms at Jill. She was sitting in the arm chair with her hands folded in her lap staring out the window. There were now snowflakes falling and the scene outside was beautiful. But I did wonder if she was okay.

I finally found a glass and filled two of them at the sink before slowly walking back to the living room. As I passed her dining table, I noticed an open box of cigars.

"Do you smoke cigars?" I asked as I sat back down on the sofa and leaned over to push a glass of water towards her.

Jill's head snapped towards me. She was

obviously confused and I had to admit I had asked out of the blue, so I tried to clarify.

"I just saw the box of cigars on the table," I said, pointing back towards the table.

"Oh, umm, I bought those for my father," Jill said. "Rich helped me by recommending which type to buy. That was before he was arrested, of course."

I nodded and sipped the water. Rich loved a good cigar and that had been his downfall apparently. Thinking of him made me feel a little down again. I tried to cheer myself up by looking out the window at the falling snow, but there was still some sort of weird vibe in the room that I couldn't get past. Besides, I needed to get back home and get back on the party prepping train.

"Are you alright Jill?" I asked quietly. I moved to the other end of the sofa so that I was closer to her. I couldn't just leave without making sure she was going to be okay. "I know the murder really threw you for a loop and I understand how scary it must have been to find out that happened just below where you live."

Jill looked away out the window and brushed a tear out of her eye. I wasn't sure what else I should do. I didn't know her that well and I wasn't sure how I could help her. The only thing I knew was that she was not okay.

"I think maybe you should find someone to

talk to," I said. "You know, just to get your feelings out."

"No!" she said. "No, I don't need that. But thank you Tessa."

She stood up in a hurry, almost knocking her glass of water over.

"I heard you are having a large party this weekend," she said. "I bet you need to go get ready."

She had a point. I stood up and grabbed the glass I had been using. I set it in the kitchen sink and put my jacket back on. When I turned back around, Jill was holding the door open for me. I walked into the hallway, but I turned and stopped her from pushing the door shut behind me.

"Hold on," I said. Jill's face looked terrified and I felt terrible. She must be always worried about someone attacking her and I've just made a sudden movement that may have been misconstrued.

"Sorry, I just wanted to ask you if you'd like to come to the party," I said. "It is a huge party and we invite half of the town. I'm sure you'll know someone there and I think it may help you cheer up a bit.

"I'll think about it," she said, her face relaxing a bit.

"Friday evening," I said. "See you there!"

I gave her a wink and a wave before turning and rushing down the stairs. Poor Jill. I wish I knew what to do to help her. I was hoping that inviting her to the party would help a little bit. I'd send her a message later in the week to invite her again. Hopefully she would agree to come. I think it would be good for her.

●Chapter Twenty-Eight●

The next two days passed by quickly as I cleaned and decorated my hind end off. I almost forgot about the murder as I busied myself with the party, but it was always there nagging at the back of my mind. I was at a stalemate. I had nothing else to look into or investigate, so I tried to push it out of my mind by listening to more true crime podcasts. I immersed myself in a different crime instead of obsessing over the one I just couldn't solve.

I invited Max over to set up for the party, but also because I needed an update on the case and how it was going. I made sure to set up something for him to do. I needed him to help me make a few cookies. Well, the cookies I was making this time were actually pretzels with almond bark poured over it and a candy coated chocolate on top. It was called "Bacon and Eggs." We always made these when I was a child and they were delicious and fun.

The best part of making these is that the first step is to pick through all of the candy coated chocolates to find the yellow ones to make the 'yolks' on the 'eggs.' We always picked out the yellow first and then the green for some silly ones. All of the rest of the candies were fair game for eating.

Max and I were sat at the table in the kitchen

with a giant bowl of candies and a cup of coffee each. We chatted a bit about town gossip as we sorted through and snacked. I hoped he would tell me about how the investigation was going, but he seemed to be steering around it.

"So, how is Rich doing?" I finally asked. "Did anything come of the new evidence I found?"

"You just like to rub that in my face, don't you?" Max said as he grinned at me.

"Yes, I kind of do," I laughed. "But I'm also just curious because I haven't heard any updates recently."

"We've been playing this one pretty close to the vest, but I will tell you because first of all, I do owe you and second of all, we are going to have this coming out in the newspaper soon enough anyway."

I nodded and waited. I was trying to work on holding my tongue a little bit because I was always amazed what people would say if I would just sit back and wait. I popped a few more candies in my mouth before I said the wrong thing.

"Well we waited to tell Rich about the new evidence," Max said. "We do that sometimes to see if they will confess or give us even more to go on. But he didn't, so we told him about the note and the charm. He didn't seem to care about the note at all, but when we told him we found a charm, he got really pale and immediately confessed."

183

"What?" I said. I had just grabbed another handful of candies, but my hand froze just above the bowl. "Rich confessed? He must have just confessed because the charm implicated Sue."

"That was our thought too," Max said with a shrug. "But there isn't much we can do. If he says he did it, we have to go with it."

I could feel the candies melting in my warm hand. It wasn't until I had popped the entire handful into my mouth that I realized I hadn't even looked through them for any yellows or greens. I stood up and went to wash the chocolate off of my hands.

"Have you talked to Sue?" I asked. "Maybe she could clarify things for you?"

"We did, but all we got out of her was that yes she had a charm bracelet. She was very emotional and she tried to say that she and Rich had been together that night, but Rich denies it."

I sighed. What in the world was going on? I was so confused by everything. I thought finding new clues would make things more clear, but so far it just made it more confusing. Each time we found something, it seemed to point to multiple people. I assumed the police were just as confused as I was.

After one more stir through the bowl of candies, it looked like we had gotten all of the yellow and green ones out. The next step was to line up the pretzels on a piece of wax paper. We need to line up pairs of the small, stick pretzels. That would be the 'bacon' in the Bacon and Egg cookies. We needed to get as many as we could on the wax paper but they couldn't be too close together or the almond bark would all run into each other and they would stick together.

I put the almond bark in the microwave to melt while Max poured us each more coffee. When I had pulled mugs out of the cabinet for us, I had picked some matching snowman mugs. One snowman was wearing a red hat, mittens, and scarf while the other was wearing blue. They had made Max roll his eyes a bit, but he was well aware of my love of all things holiday and put up with it well.

Once the almond bark was melted, I poured a small spoonful over the middle of each pretzel pair and then Max pushed a candy into it before it hardened. We made a good team and before long, all of the cookies were sitting to harden. I plucked up the first two we had made and gave one to Max so we could appreciate all of our hard work.

We sat back down at the table to finish our coffee. Max had to be back at work in about an hour, so he wouldn't be able to help me much more, but I did have one more question for him that I'd thought of while we were working.

"So who do you actually think did it?" I asked. "Did Sue do it and Rich is covering for her? Or did

Rich do it and Sue is trying to help him?"

"Your guess is as good as mine at this point," Max said with a shrug. He drained the rest of his coffee mug. "Honestly, sometimes it feels like neither of them did it and sometimes it feels like both of them did it. I have no idea what to make of it and I just keep hoping we will stumble on something else that will clear things up."

I nodded. So the police were on the same page that I was. And now Rich would be tried for murder because he confessed for something he may not have even done. What an awful situation this was turning out to be.

I walked Max to the front door and after waving him off down the driveway, I glanced over the decorations. Everything in the entry seemed to be in place and cheery. I tried to push the murder out of my head again as I admired the evergreen garland draped around the front door and the mistletoe I had hung in the doorway to the living room.

The party was tomorrow and even though we were having most of it catered this year, I still had plenty of things to make. We always had trays of homemade cookies that needed to be baked. I rolled up my sleeves and went back to the kitchen to move on to the next batch.

•Chapter Twenty-Nine•

After making four more types of cookies, with a little help from Trina and Tank when he got home from school, the cookies were done and ready to be set out for the party. The next order of business was to check on Mandy and her progress on the donuts we had ordered for the party.

Trina went back to desk duty and Tank headed in to the Christmas Shop for his shift while I drove to the Donut Hut. Technically, it was closed for the day now because it was only open through lunch. But I parked in the alley and went in through the kitchen door to see how Mandy was doing.

On one of the large, rolling racks that she had there were trays and trays of donuts that I walked over to inspect after hanging up my jacket. Each tray was decorated with a different sort of holiday style. I saw a rack of red frosted donuts with green sprinkles and a rack of green frosted donuts with red sprinkles. There were also donuts decorated like wreaths and long john donuts with white frosting and little seasonal sprinkles on top. I started to reach for one of the donuts to taste it when Mandy spoke up.

"No, no, no," she said without even looking up from her frosting. "Don't you dare take one of those donuts. I know you ordered them, but I don't have

187

any to spare."

I guiltily pulled my hand back and went to check the coffee pot. Mandy knew I would be coming and she had a hot carafe of decaf coffee ready and waiting. I didn't care how caffeinated the coffee was, I would drink it no matter what time of day it was. Mandy was just looking out for my best interests and making sure I'd be able to get the sleep I desperately needed that night. I poured two mugs and walked them over to where the stools were under the island.

"Are you able to stop and take a break?" I asked.

"Yeah, I'm good for a little while," she said as she frosted one last donut.

Mandy sat down with me and over a cup of decaf, I told her about everything Max had told me: the new evidence, Rich's confession, and Sue's insistence that she had an alibi for him. The entire time, Mandy sipped her coffee and listened intently until I was finished.

"So, what are your thoughts?" Mandy asked when I got to the end.

"I have no idea," I said with a sigh. "I've gotten to the point where I feel like I can't even think about it anymore because I've exhausted everything. Every time I think I've figured it out, a new clue pops up and proves me wrong. The evidence I keep finding implicates multiple people. We know there was only one killer, but both of them seem guilty."

"Could it have been someone besides Rich or Sue?" she asked. Mandy was great at playing the nagging voice in my head.

"I suppose so, but I'm not really sure who," I said. "It's been hard to think of other suspects when Rich and Sue are so out there with their evidence and alibis and confessions."

I drank some more decaf coffee and let Mandy turn our conversation towards the upcoming holidays. As always, I would be at home with all of the members of my family from my grandma who comes into town all the way down to my newest niece, who was almost a year old. Mandy would be headed to Florida for a week to visit her parents and the Donut Hut would be closed during that time. I had already made her promise she would pre-make me one donut for each day she would be gone, not that I really needed them.

"Shoot," I said as the talk of the holiday brought something back to my mind. "I was going to ask Jill if she would possibly make some necklaces for my sisters and my mother. She was acting so weird the other day that I totally forgot. I need to message her."

"Why don't you message her now," Mandy said. "I need to move these trays of donuts into the fridge to keep for the night."

I grabbed my flip phone out of my purse and sat down to type out a message while Mandy slowly wheeled the big rack of trays away. I hoped that Jill would be able to help me because I knew my family would love to get a necklace from Jill. I was slightly worried because she had been so out of it the other day. I didn't know if it would help or hurt to have something like this to work on.

Hey Jill, I was going to ask you the other day if I'd be able to commission a few necklaces from you for my sisters and mother. Please let me know soon but bon't feel obligated if there isn't time to get them done before the holidays because then I'll commission a few for their birthdays instead.

I flipped my phone shut and waited for Mandy to get back into the kitchen. I could hear her banging around in the walk-in freezer. My phone buzzed and I was pleased to see that Jill had gotten right back to me.

I certainly have time for you after all of your kindness. Let me know what you're thinking for each one ASAP and I'll get working.

Mandy shut the door to the walk-in and came back to sit on the stool next to her. I told her that Jill had agreed and I asked her what she thought I should ask for. Mandy had a much better fashion sense than I did. Together, we agreed that Trina would love a necklace with interlocking hearts to symbolize her and her fiance. Tilly would probably like something to symbolize her three children. And my mother loved Christmas so much that I thought she might like a larger wire Christmas tree with some red and green ornaments on it. I texted all of that information to Jill and was pleased that Jill said she could have them ready soon.

I may not be solving a murder, but I was planning an epic holiday party and getting all of the presents sorted. Maybe this time I would have to leave the police work to the police.

•Chapter Thirty•

Friday morning dawned and like it or not, I had a party to throw that night. My father and I helped my mother come down the stairs first thing so that she could station herself in the middle of the party prep. She may not have been much help initially, but she was going to have a hand in all of the last minute preparations. I also knew that my mother felt bad because she had spent the last few days trying to rest up so that she was able to make it through the party.

"You did a great job of decorating, Tessa," she exclaimed once we got her onto the couch in the living room. "This all looks amazing and I think the party will go swimmingly."

"Thank you Mom, but I still have a little ways to go," I said. "I have a surprise for you and I was going to wait until tonight, but I need your advice. I've gotten the high school jazz band to come and play Christmas carols for us tonight, but I need a place for them to set up. Maybe you and Dad could figure out exactly where to put them?"

My mother clapped her hands together and my father cracked a smile. If there was something my mother loved, it was a great, big surprise. I knew she would never see a surprise band coming.

"That's a wonderful surprise," my mother exclaimed. "I can't believe I hadn't thought of that all of these years that I've been throwing this party. I'm pleased you thought of it though. Maybe soon I'll have to let you plan this party every year."

My shock must have shown on my face because my mother and father both burst out laughing. I laughed along with them. Party planning was stressful. But planning a party all about Christmas, one of my most favorite things in the world, made it so much more enjoyable.

As my mother looked around the room from her perch on the couch muttering to herself about where to seat a live band, I went into the kitchen to see how things were going. Mandy had come first thing in the morning with the boxes of donuts and I started to put them out on the individual trays.

My father came through the swinging doors of the kitchen and stood next to me, shifting his weight from side to side. I could tell he had something to tell me that I probably didn't want to hear.

"Umm, Tessa," he said nervously. "I know you were going to try to save the jazz band for the surprise, but I had kind of told your mother that you would have a big surprise for her tonight and now you've spoiled it so she is going to be pretty upset. Remember how much your mother loves surprises?"

Oh shoot, yeah I did remember that. One time

193

we tried to plan a surprise trip for her and my father for their anniversary and Tank had accidentally let it slip and my mother cried because it wasn't a surprise anymore. Surprises were a big, big deal for her. She wasn't a very demanding woman, but she just really loved surprises.

"I was wondering if maybe there is something else we could do for a surprise for her?" my father asked. "It doesn't have to be big, just something special for a surprise."

I thought for a moment as I finished arranging the donuts and then covering the trays with a tea towel. I had an idea, but I wasn't sure if I would be able to do it or not.

"Do you think a necklace would be enough of a surprise?" I asked my father. "A nice, handmade, Christmas style necklace?"

"Oh that would be a beautiful surprise," my father said. "You know she likes to wear that black dress for the party and a holiday necklace would look lovely I think."

"I agree that it would look lovely," I said. "Now the biggest problem is making sure I can get it today. I asked Jill to make it and she's only had two days, so I'm not sure it'll be done. I'll have to go sweet talk her and see what I can do."

"Thank you so much," my father said. "After she got over her delight about the jazz band, she immediately started to lament the ruined surprise. I was really worried I'd have to hear about the ruined surprise for ages, but this necklace will definitely help."

My father bustled out of the kitchen to go help my mother and I finished covering up the trays of donuts before I pulled out my phone to message Jill again. I figured I'd need to ask for the rush order in person.

Hi Jill, I hate to ask, but are you free to meet today? I have a huge favor to ask you.

As I waited for her to message me back, I sat down and made a list of all the things that needed to be done before the party so that even though I had to leave on an errand, other members of the Schmidt family could continue set-up.

The list grew longer and longer with things like picking up the catering order, setting up the catering order, setting up tables for the food, setting up tables for people to sit, and now setting up an area for the jazz band. There was a lot to do, but I knew I would be extremely happy once the party was in full swing and everyone was having fun.

As I finished up the list and brought it out of the kitchen, my phone buzzed in my pocket. I took it out and glanced at the message, which was from Jill.

I am free. Come on over anytime.

I found Trina in the living room with my

mother and decided to put her in charge of the list because if I gave it to my father, the list would inevitably get lost. I went through the list with them so they knew what each thing was and told them I needed to run an errand, but would be back soon enough.

I knew the favor I needed to ask Jill for was a pretty big one, so I swung by the Donut Hut for a little treat to sweeten the deal. Mandy happened to remember that Jill's favorite donut was just a plain old round, glazed donut so she packed me up two of them and some to-go coffees for both Jill and I.

It wasn't a very cold day, so I decided to walk over to Jill's apartment since it was just a block away. It was just cold enough to snow, but there was no wind. The snow fell softly straight down and it felt almost like I was in a movie. If only I could stop and enjoy it a bit more, but I pushed on so that I could get back to the party. There would be time to appreciate the holidays more when the holiday party was over.

•Chapter Thirty-One•

This time when Jill opened her apartment door, she seemed to be back to herself. She smiled and greeted me right away and I was hoping that meant she was starting to come out the other side of the dark place she had been in. She grabbed one of the cups of coffee out of my hand. I stepped inside and set the donuts on the table. As I took my jacket off, Jill got out two plates.

We took our donuts and coffee into the living room and sat back in the same places we had been in three days ago. I was a little nervous about asking her for such a big favor, so I decided to start off with a little chit-chat.

"Did you see the beautiful snow outside today?" I asked as if somehow she would have missed the snow falling outside of the gigantic windows next to us. I just couldn't help myself. As a life-long Minnesotan, weather is our go--to conversation starter.

"Yes, isn't it lovely?" Jill said. She had a giant smile on his face which seemed almost manic. I'm not sure what she was smiling about exactly, but I was glad to see any emotion play on her face.

"Do you have a plan for the holidays?" I asked.

"Oh yes, I'm headed back to my hometown up

north to spend some time with my parents," she said. "Same old same old, but I am excited."

She certainly seemed excited. Jill was fidgeting so much she was almost vibrating. As we had our donuts and coffee she kept shifting around in her chair and pushing her hair behind her ears. I decided it was time to spring my question on her. She was obviously in a good enough mood and I was running out of things to talk about because I didn't know her that well.

"I'll get to the point of why I'm here," I said. "I accidentally ruined a surprise for my mother and I'd like to make it up to her tonight by giving her another surprise. So I was wondering if there was anyway you could finished the necklace for her by the party tonight? I know it's asking a lot."

"Of course I can," she said. "Actually I have it mostly done already, so I'll just finish it up quickly and you can surprise your mother tonight."

I smiled while I gave a big sigh and sank back into the itchy sofa with my coffee. What an absolute relief for me. My mother would be so pleased tonight to be given that beautiful necklace. As I happily sipped my coffee, Jill sat looking at me with the big smile still on her face. She was holding her coffee mug in her hands and just staring at me, which was a bit off-putting.

Suddenly an idea popped into my head and I

debated whether I should go with it or not. As much as I wanted to forget about the murder, I just couldn't. Jill had been right here, above the murder when it happened. The last time we had been together, she had been so melancholy I didn't dare ask. Today, though, she was in such a good mood that I decided I could at least broach the subject.

"Jill, I have a hard question I'd like to ask you but you don't need to answer if you don't want to," I said.

Jill cocked her head at me like a dog when they don't understand. She still had a smile on her face as she answered.

"Go ahead," she said. I was sure she knew that it would be about the murder.

"You were up here when Claire was murdered downstairs, right?" I asked. "Did you hear anything?"

Jill's eyes opened wide and her fidgeting stopped. Immediately I regretted asking her because I was afraid that she would slide back into the dark place she had been living in for so long. But after a moment, the smile appeared on her face again.

"I was up here, but I didn't hear anything," she said. Jill's dark eyes bored into me. "If I had heard something, I would have called, don't you think? I am a single woman who lives up here alone. If I had thought anything sordid was happening downstairs, I would not have hesitated to call for help. Isn't that what you would have done?"

I nodded at her. She seemed to be asking me rather than telling me, which seemed a bit odd. But while I could understand being defensive about something so dark and depraved, it did confuse me. I was positive that Claire did not die quickly so she would have definitely had time to call loudly for help or scream at the murderer. And in an old building like this she would have been sure to hear that.

"Are you sure?" I asked. "It just seems so weird that you wouldn't have heard Claire call for help."

"I'm sure," Jill said. The smile had fallen from her face and her eyes were burning into me like hot pokers. I immediately regretted asking her again and I knew that I needed to be done with the questioning. Besides, I needed to get back to party prep.

I popped the last piece of the donut in front of me into my mouth and grabbed my plate as I stood up.

"I really should be going," I said. "I have a lot to do when I get home to set up for the party. By the way, are you coming to the party? You really should because you need to get me that necklace anyways."

Jill turned and stared off into space for a moment and I wondered for a moment if she had somehow not heard me. I put my plate in the kitchen sink and put my jacket on. As I was about to just let myself out, Jill stood up and joined me at the door.

"I'll come to deliver the necklace, but I'm not sure I'll stay for the party," Jill said. "I'm not sure how I'm feeling right now if I am honest."

"Well we would love to have you," I said with a smile. "And I'm sorry I brought the murder up again. I can see that it is something that really affects you."

Jill stared at me for another moment before she gave one big nod and silently opened the door for me.

"Come by whenever to drop off the necklace and please consider staying," I said. Jill nodded curtly again at me and as soon as I was through the doorway, she slammed the apartment door behind me.

I was thankful that she had agreed to finishing the necklace. That would make the party even better. But speaking of the party, I needed to get going to make sure the preparations had been humming along without me. I was practically counting down the hours until the party started and I could be done worrying about it, for this year at least.

•Chapter Thirty-Two•

I had been happily surprised to arrive home to find that the party preparations were in full swing so there wasn't as much to be done. I had expected the worst when I pulled up to the house, but Trina and my dad had been dutifully crossing things off of the list.

As soon as I finished up a few more things, I went upstairs to get ready. I wasn't much of a fashionista, but Mandy had helped me put together a nice outfit for the night. I put on a nice pair of tight, black leggings and a forest green tunic top that looked great with my dark hair and pale skin. I had a necklace with large red beads to really play up the Christmas theme without being too childish. I swiped on a bit more makeup than normal and put my hair up in a low, loose side bun. I took one more look in the mirror and smiled at myself.

When I was younger, I had been so self-critical of my appearance and my complete inability to figure out how to do my hair and makeup didn't my critique of myself at all. But now at the tender age of thirty and after being through many trials of life, I had accepted myself and actually loved myself as I should have my entire life. I was able to think that not only did I look okay, I actually looked good.

Coming down the stairs, I was almost overcome with holiday spirit. The halls were absolutely decked and the dining room was full of the appetizers and desserts. I was so pleased and I hoped my mother would be also. When Tank carried her down the stairs just behind me, I could tell from the smile on her face that she was so happy and excited for the party.

"Oh Tessa, this is amazing!" she exclaimed as Tank put her in the wheelchair we had borrowed for the party. My mother had said there was no way she would be stuck on the couch during the entire party.

The doorbell rang and I sent Tank over to let the jazz band in and show them where they were going to set up for the night. He went to school with them and he was well-liked, which was evidenced by the individual greeting he gave each smiling member that walked in clutching their instrument case.

One member of the jazz band in particular was greeted with a large, shy smile. Judging by the guitar case the girl was carrying, I suspected that must be Angie. I caught Tank's eye and winked, which made him blush furiously.

As the clock ticked closer and closer to the party start time, I walked nervous circles around the main floor: checking the food tables, checking my mother, checking the jazz band, looking out the front window and repeat. If I kept that up for long, I'd preburn off all of the calories I was about to ingest at the party.

Finally on one of my loops, I saw Clark's old pickup truck pulling into the driveway. I put my nervous circles on hold and waited at the front door for him to make his way up. As he got up to the porch, I whipped the front door open just as he lifted his hand to knock. He chuckled at my total inability to be chill and I showed him in the door and to where we had a rack set up to hang up jackets.

"I think we need to go find you a drink," he said as I also noticed that I was nervously wringing my hands.

"I just can't help it," I said. "I want everything to be prefect. My mom always throws an amazing, fantastic holiday party and I need mine to live up to hers."

"Not that I've been to your mother's party," Clark said, "but this one looks pretty great."

He steered me towards the mistletoe that hung in the doorway to the living room and I let him, even though my mother's wheelchair was currently parked in there. She was distracted by the jazz band, who were tuning their instruments and warming up in the corner.

Clark gave me a quick, but passion-filled kiss which spread warmth all the way down to my toes and made me hope that my mother really hadn't been looking. I stumbled backward a step and Clark put out his hand to steady me, a sly smile on his face. It took me a moment to regain my composure, but when I did I pulled him with me towards the bar area.

We had offered to pay Trina to tend bar and she happily agreed. When Clark and I walked over, she already had a glass of white wine waiting for me on the table in front of her.

"I've been watching you pace for half an hour," she said as she handed me the glass. "I poured this about halfway through that because I knew you'd be over soon enough."

As Trina got a beer for Clark, Max came in through the front door. I looked at Clark and jerked my head towards Max. Clark nodded and struck up a conversation with Trina about school while I went to greet Max. I gave him a big hug and helped him hang up his jacket.

"I'm so glad you didn't have to work tonight," I said. "I'm just hoping everything goes alright."

"Everything looks great," Max said as he gave me a peck on the cheek.

"Thank you," I said. "That means a lot from someone who has been at so many Schmidt Christmas parties in the past. Not to ruin the festive mood, but I did want to ask if you have learned anything else about Rich?"

"Nope," Max said, with a guilty shrug. I could tell that it was wearing on him also, but there wasn't anything he could do about it. "I wish something would turn up, but it's been so long since the murder now that I'm not sure we will find anything else."

The awkward silence hung between us for a few moments. I knew we both wished that things would turn out differently for him. But our hands were tied, each for different reasons. I was just a concerned citizen that was snooping around and he had to follow the rules of the police department. We stared at each other and Max gave my hand a little squeeze.

"It looks like you already have a drink, but I sure could use one," Max said finally. He stuck out his elbow towards me. "Would you mind accompanying me to the bar?"

I looped my arm through his and walked through the foyer over to where Clark and Trina were still chatting about college. Trina was a junior in college and had decided to go into education, so she and Clark were talking about the ins and outs of getting an education degree.

When we walked up, Trina pulled out another bottle of beer for him. She had known him so long that she didn't even have to ask him which kind he would like. Even after I gotten married and moved away, Max had stayed almost like a brother to my younger siblings.

Suddenly, I remembered that Jill was going to deliver the necklace. I knew that I would have a lot of things going on and Trina would have a great view of the door. I needed her to keep an eye out for me.

"Trina, I know you will be a little busy, but I have a huge favor to ask you," I said. "Jill will be coming over with something she needs to give me. Don't let Mom see her because it is a present for her. But let me know so I can get it and surprise Mom."

"Ooooooh, did you get Mom a necklace?" Trina squealed, loud enough that I glanced around to make sure Mom hadn't rolled up behind me. "That will be an awesome present. I love the jewelry that Jill makes."

I chalked up a victory in the gift area since Trina would also be receiving her own necklace in a few more weeks. My sisters were notoriously hard to shop for, so I was pleased to hear that Trina would enjoy her present.

"I'm surprised Jill said she would make then necklace," Max said. "She was really shaken up after the murder. We could hardly interview her about it, even a few days after the fact."

"I've actually gone to see her twice now," I said. "The first time she was just like you described. She just kept staring off into space and she was emotionless. But I went to see her yesterday and she had perked up considerably. Obviously she didn't want to discuss the murder, but..."

"You asked her about the murder?" Max exclaimed.

"Oh Tessa, you didn't," Trina said.

Clark just sighed and shook his head at me.

I have to admit that when I said it out loud like that, it did sound like a terrible thing to do. I considered trying to explain myself, but I knew I could never make them see what I really meant. It wasn't like I had just blurted it out when I was talking to Jill or something. That needed to be put in the past and fast. So I was glad to hear the jazz band starting to play a few practice songs. I grabbed my wine glass and made my way towards the living room.

"Come on boys," I said. "I'm headed to listen to some good music and get this party started."

The front door opened as I passed and I stopped to greet a few people from town before my father came to take over greeting duty. As I watched, people came in and grabbed food and drinks before mingling around with smiles on their faces. The party seemed to be off to a good start. I finally felt like I could relax a little bit.

•Chapter Thirty-Three•

The party was in full swing and I was starting to get a little bit worried that Jill wasn't going to come. I knew she hadn't been totally on board with actually staying to attend the party, but I was pretty sure I remembered her saying she would come to drop the necklace off.

I pulled my flip phone out of my pocket and looked at it again. Nothing new. I figured that if something happened and she wasn't going to come, that she would at least let me know. I debated whether I should message her, but I felt I had already been demanding enough asking for the necklace to be finished in such a short time frame. My Minnesota nice may be extending a bit too far. I told myself that I would get one more glass of wine and if I hadn't heard from her by then, that I would message her instead.

The walk from the living room to the bar was short, but took a while because I was stopped by no less than ten people. Chelsea even gave me a half-smile as I walked by a group of people she was sitting with. I briefly wondered how in the world she had been invited, but that was not in the Christmas spirit, so I gave her a little wave.

Ronald had brought his dour wife Melinda and

they had somehow taken over greeting duty. I guess it was only natural to want to greet everyone when you are the mayor and you are up for re-election in the next year.

"Tessa, what an amazing party," Ronald said. Today, the sweater vest stretched over his large stomach was Christmas themed with reindeer running back and forth across it "Your mother tells me you put all of this together. If that is true, I may have to get your help with more of the town events."

"The music is too loud," Melinda said, her face permanently pulled up into a sneer.

"Well thank you Ronald," I said, ignoring Melinda. She may not be a fun person to be around, but she loved Ronald and he loved her. Together, they made a strange duo that just worked. "Maybe I will help you with some other town events, but for now, I'm headed towards the bar. Do you or Melinda need anything?"

Ronald opened his mouth and started to say something, but Melinda cut him off with a subtle karate chop to the stomach.

"No, we do not need the extra calories in any sort of alcoholic beverage," Melinda said.

The front door opened and she turned back towards it to scowl at whoever was the next to arrive. Ronald chuckled as he shrugged a little bit. What we all saw as Melinda's fatal flaw, he somehow embraced in an 'aw shucks' sort of way. Honestly, it made me believe in true love.

"Thank you for offering Tessa," Ronald said before turning to save the unsuspecting guests who had walked in to Melinda's laser beam like glare. I noticed that one of the reindeer on the back of his sweater had a red nose and it made me smile to myself.

I turned to make my way to the bar when I thought I heard someone calling my name. I turned and saw Jill shuffling by Ronald and Melinda's greetings. She had on a large, purple, puffy winter coat and a big knit hat that was covered in snowflakes. She was carrying a big box in her hands, a box that was almost as big as the ones Mandy put a dozen donuts in at the Donut Hut. It confused me a bit because the necklace certainly didn't need a box that big. But I had mentioned that the necklace was going to be a surprise, so maybe she was just playing along. I was a bit touched by her thoughtfulness.

"Jill, I'm so glad you made it," I said, rushing forward to take the box out of her hands.

She wrenched the box back and clutched it tightly against the front of her big purple coat.

"I'm only here for a few moments," she said quietly. "I won't be staying for the party."

"What a shame," I said, a bit too exuberantly. I realized in that moment that I had imbibed with one glass of wine too many and I was glad I hadn't been able to reach the bar again yet. I promised myself I would grab some food next, and not just a cookie or donut.

"Can we go somewhere quiet?" Jill asked. "Maybe upstairs?"

"Oh sure but I'll need you to take your boots off," I said, gesturing to the big black, fur-lined boots she was wearing. It looked like she had trudged through ankle deep, muddy snow and I did not want that tracked through the house.

Jill hesitated for a moment, looking down at her feet and biting her lip like she was pondering something. I put my hands out again to offer to take the box from her.

"Why don't I hold that while you take your boots off?"

"No!" she shouted, and then looking embarrassed, brought her voice back down to speak softly again. "I can do it."

I wasn't really sure why she was so adamant about holding the box, but I let her. I reminded myself that she was still in a delicate state and she needed to be supported, not chastised. So I watched while she clutched the box against herself and tried to take her boots off by stepping one at a time on the backs of the boots. Finally, she was in her stocking feet and stared at me until I beckoned her to follow me.

212

As we started up the stairs to the second floor, we left the din of the crowd below. With every step, the conversations and music faded a bit more into the background. The hallway only had a touch of holiday decorating because I had focused my attention on the first floor. But on the door to our private, family area was a wreath. I had tried to infuse a little holiday spirit.

Our apartment itself needed more holiday cheer and I was planning to have my siblings come over soon to help me put up the family tree. But for now, it just looked like a normal, Midwestern home. I knew my mother wouldn't be able to surprise us in here because of the obvious problem with stairs, but I didn't want my sisters to come in. I assumed the reason for the large box may be that she had finished all three necklaces. So instead of just having her come to the living room, I brought her all the way to my bedroom.

"You can take off your jacket," I said as we walked in. "I know you aren't staying, but you must be awfully hot."

"I'm fine," Jill said. She shut my bedroom door behind her and stood directly in front of it. "I really do have to leave right after I give you this."

She gingerly lifted the box a bit to indicate what she was talking about. I was a bit confused about why she was still being so cryptic. We were in privacy now.

"Okay, you don't have to stay," I said, taking a step towards her. "You can just give me the necklace and go back home."

"The necklace?" Jill said. Her hand flew to her throat and wrapped around a necklace she was wearing before she loosened her grip. "Oh, yeah the necklace for your mother."

I took another step towards Jill and put my hand out towards her. She flinched and jerked the box away from me again. I was getting a bit worried about her mental state.

"Jill, are you okay?" I asked.

"Not really," she said. "But I will be after this. Right now, I need you to go sit on the bed while I open the box."

I complied, walking over and perching on the edge of the bed. An uneasy feeling was starting to settle in my gut, but I tried to ignore that. It was obvious that Jill needed help, but how could I help her? I needed to find a way.

•Chapter Thirty-Four•

For a while, Jill stood by the door with the box in her hands just staring at me. She was pale and sweaty and she looked like she was almost ready to pass out. I sat uneasily on the very edge of the bed, ready to spring up and catch her if she started to faint and fall down. I wished she would take that jacket off, but I'd already asked her a few times and she seemed to be getting angry, so I didn't want to push it.

"How long have you been making necklaces Jill?" I asked. I was hoping to break the tension by getting her to talk about something she enjoyed. "They are so beautiful and you really are wonderful at it. Do you make anything for yourself?"

"Thank you," Jill said, her face brightening a bit. "Yes, I actually made the one that I am wearing and it means a lot to me. Would you like to see?"

She grabbed the necklace from around her neck and slipped it off over her head. I put my hand out and she dropped it into my palm. I noticed a glint of gold inside the wrist of her jacket as she pulled her hand back. Jill was wearing some sort of a gold bracelet.

I looked down. The gold chain of the necklace had a little gold, wire charm on it in the shape of a horse. It was small, only the size of marble, but somehow it was filled with detail. It wasn't just a charm shaped kind of like a horse, it was a horse charm. The thin wire had been twisted back and forth delicately until it had come out just perfectly.

"Do you like horses?" I asked. My mind flashed back to the picture of a horse she had in her apartment. "I noticed you have a picture of one in your apartment."

"I've always loved horses," Jill said. "I wanted to ride horses all of my life, but we were too poor. I finally had to take matters into my own hands. I found a way to buy a horse that I loved when I was only sixteen, but unfortunately we had to put Misty down just a few years after. I have been too heartbroken to get another horse since then."

Jill started to cry. I turned and grabbed a box of tissues off of my nightstand and handed one to her along with her necklace. She slipped the necklace back over her head and dabbed at her eyes with the tissue before blowing her nose with a loud honk.

For a minute, I stared at her. Despite having been to her apartment twice now, I still didn't know much about Jill. She seemed to be about my age, but otherwise I didn't know where she was from or why she had moved here. She was quiet and kept to herself. I had always scoffed at the idea that it was hard to make friends when moving to a small town. Small towns are always friendly, I thought, just look at Shady Lake. I can't go anywhere without being recognized and talked to by someone.

But here was proof. Jill seemed nice and yet almost a year after she had moved here, we didn't know hardly anything about her. The reason Shady Lake had been so welcoming and comfortable for me was because I had grown up here. But it takes a while for us to accept strangers like Jill, no matter how nice their jewelry was.

"This might seem kind of weird but I do want to apologize," I said. Jill gave me a strange look, but I plowed on. "I just realized that even though we are the same age and you've been here for a while, I never really tried to talk to you much or be your friend. I'm so sorry. I assume no one was very welcoming since I hardly know anything about you."

Jill sighed a big sigh and dabbed at her eyes again with the wadded up tissue. I offered her a new one from the box, which she gladly pulled out and also used. She set down the box on the desk next to her. I eyed it up, but it still just looked like a large white box to me.

"This may sound strange, but I kind of liked the peace and quiet," Jill said. "I moved to Shady Lake for a fresh start and I really wanted some place where I could start fresh. Shady Lake provided just that, although it was a bit lonely. I got over that by being extra friendly while waitressing. That way I did get some social interaction."

"Well I'm still sorry," I said. "I'd love if you told me a little more about yourself."

"I grew up in a very small town up north," Jill said. She was facing my direction, but she was staring out of the window next to me where the snow was softly falling, making the Christmas party feel so cozy. "The town I'm from is way smaller than here and I always dreamed of living in the big city. I always wanted a fancy life in a great apartment."

She chuckled to herself and she seemed to be lost in her childhood dreams, smiling at how ridiculous and wonderful they were all at once. I knew how she felt because I felt that way too when I thought back to my desire to be a 'fashionable lady' when I grew up. That obviously hadn't happened, but my ideas about it were still there in the back of my mind.

"I've been making necklaces since I was a teenager," Jill said. "My parents didn't have any money and if I ever wanted anything, I had to make the money for it myself. So I started making jewelry and it just kept getting better and better. In fact before I moved here, I sold my stuff in boutiques all over the Cities. I was making a good living as an artist."

She was looking off into the distance and her eyes almost seemed to glaze over. It was like she was dreaming about her former life. I knew what it was

like to have two different lives. She had been a
working artist in a big city and now here she was
waitressing in a small town. While my move from one
world to another had been good despite the
circumstances, I got the feeling that her move was not
so happy and plucky as mine turned out to be.

"You were making a good living as an artist?" I
asked. "What happened?"

Jill turned to me with a sneer on her face. Her
eyes were blazing angrily and her pale face suddenly
turned red. All of the happiness and wonder that had
been there when she talked about her childhood
dreams had been pulled off and thrown to the side.

"What happened was that ugly witch Claire
accused me of stealing," Jill said. "Suddenly all of my
jewelry was on clearance and no more orders were
coming in. All of the other boutique owners were her
friends. They weren't going to turn their backs on her,
so they turned their backs on me instead."

I sat up straighter as I took in what she had
said. I replayed her words in my head a few times
while she appeared to be lost in the painful memories
of the past. It was like the curtain had suddenly
dropped and I wasn't quite sure what I was taking in.

"Wait a minute," I said. "You knew Claire
before she came down to the shop that day?"

"I've known Claire for years," Jill said. She was
yelling now, but I knew no one could probably hear

her over the noise of the party. "Claire was the one who discovered my work and befriended me. She owned her own store and wanted to sell my necklaces and other jewelry there. She convinced me that my work was good and could be sold for much higher prices than what I was selling them for. She helped me get my jewelry into all of the other boutiques."

I sat uneasily on the bed. Jill was agitated and was pacing in front of my bedroom door. As long as she stayed where she was, I was trapped. I decided to just be as quiet and unassuming as possible. I couldn't afford to make her angrier.

"I was living the high life and Claire was my best friend," Jill said. "We were on the society pages of the newspaper and I was invited to the biggest and best parties. I was finally living the life I had dreamed of as a child growing up in a trailer."

Jill paused her story, her eyes shining. I could almost see the memories of those parties scrolling through her head like a slideshow.

"So what happened then?" I asked. I knew I was tempting fate, but I couldn't just sit there and stare at her.

"A lot of the boutiques where I sold my jewelry started to get money stolen from them," Jill said. "They weren't large robberies, but stealing a few hundred dollars from a small boutique is quite a hit, so it was a big deal. Claire accused me of it and turned everyone against me. She said that since I was trailer trash, I was obviously the culprit."

Her face fell and she looked like a child who had just had their dreams crushed. I suppose that she kind of was. She had been living her dream life and it had fallen down all around her despite her hard work.

"I'm so sorry Jill," I said. "That is awful."

"What hurts even more is that after she turned everyone against me, she caught the actual thief red-handed," Jill said. "Another artist who showcased and sold her shirts in the boutiques had fallen into a drug habit and started to steal from the registers when she came by to drop off her orders."

I didn't even know what to say to Jill. I stood up and walked over to put my hand on her arm. For a moment, she let it stay there. But then she shook her head like she was coming out of a fog and she pushed my hand off as she backed towards the desk where she had set the box down.

"It was too late by then," Jill said. "All of the boutique owners had moved on and my name had been slandered all over town. I knew I needed a fresh start, so I just packed up my car and drove."

"You drove until you got to Shady Lake," I said. "I understand why you wanted the peace and quiet."

"And I had that until Claire walked into the
221

Christmas Shop that day," Jill said.

"But I was there, Claire didn't even seem to recognize you," I said, confused because Claire had given no indication that she had known who anyone in the room was.

"She did and she came to my door later that afternoon to try to apologize," Jill said. "But I wasn't about to let her get off so easy. I had seen her true self and it was ugly. I knew someone had to do something."

Jill's tone had dropped into a serious and sinister place. She was still standing in front of the only exit and, if what I was starting to think was true, I knew that I had gotten myself into real trouble.

•Chapter Thirty-Five•

Jill turned around and grabbed the top off of the white box. I couldn't see what was inside and suddenly I was quite aware that it was probably not the necklaces I had ordered. My mind spun and I tried to figure out what to do. Unfortunately, the glasses of wine I had consumed in celebration of the party were now slowing down my thought processes.

"I feel so honored that you told me all of that," I said. I stood up and walked towards Jill and the door. "I promise that it can just be a secret between you and I. No one else has to know."

"No one else will know," she said. "And you can yell all you want, but no one can hear you over the noise of the party. It really did work out perfectly for you to invite me here."

Jill reached into the box and pulled out a pistol that she pointed at me. I immediately backed away which unfortunately meant I was also backing away from the door. Jill's hand was shaking while she threatened me.

"You were the one that killed Claire," I said. My voice was shaking. Everything seemed to be falling into place now.

"I thought I had covered all of my tracks," Jill said. "I was so careful about everything and I even

223

planned a few things to help. It helped that I lived above the crime scene so I was able to go up and grab some things to stage the crime."

"Wait," I exclaimed. Jill leveled her gun at me again. "If I am going to die anyways, I deserve an explanation. I understand why you killed her, but how did you cover your tracks so thoroughly?"

Jill laughed a maniacal laugh. Her eyes darted all over the room, but her gun always stayed pointed right at me. I didn't dare make any sudden movements or I was afraid she would pull the trigger.

"As if you didn't already know!" she exclaimed.

Apparently she thought I had already solved everything and had simply not turned her in yet. While I appreciated that she thought I was so smart, I really didn't know. Jill had not really been on my radar besides the fact that she had been acting strange.

And she was still acting strange. Here she was pacing in front of the door with a pistol pointed at me. That would certainly qualify as strange.

"Okay, fine," she said. "I'll spell it all out for you. After the confrontation at the store, Clarie came to my apartment that afternoon to apologize to me. I wouldn't even let her in. I laughed in her face because she had ruined my life! Did she really think she could just waltz back in and apologize and everything would be hunky-dory?"

Now, I hadn't really known Claire, but from my brief time with her I got the impression that yes, she did think that it would set everything straight. Claire had seemed like the kind of person allowed to do whatever she wanted whenever she wanted to do that. Of course, that didn't mean she should have been murdered.

"Anyways, I did feel kind bad and figured I should meet her to hear her out," Jill said. "So after she left, I dropped off that note telling her to meet me that night. When she came over, she thought we could go back to being friends. I told her that I had been really hurt by her, especially when she called me trailer trash. But she laughed again. She laughed at me and told me that she had just been telling the truth and that I shouldn't be ashamed of where I came from. That I should accept it, own it, and move on."

As Jill talked, her eyes were filling with tears again. This time, she didn't wipe them away. She just let them flow down her cheeks as she waved the gun around while she gestured. I hadn't liked Claire from just that small encounter at the Christmas Shop and judging by Jill's story, there was no hidden, redeeming factor that would have made me like her even more.

Obviously I don't ever condone murder, but I really felt for Jill in that moment. She had worked so hard to achieve her childhood dreams and all it took was one selfish person to rip them away. And then she had moved away to try to rebuild. I didn't blame her for being angry when Claire came to town. I felt bad for Jill and then I caught a glimpse of the gun again and remembered she was kind of planning on killing me.

"At that moment, I decided I needed to do something," she said. "So I told her I could let her into the Christmas Shop. I couldn't just kill her in my apartment. Then it would be obvious it was me. I felt bad because I really did like Sue, but it couldn't be helped. So I took her down there and walked through the dark store with her. Sue had left her keys in the door as she does more often than she remembers them, so I didn't even have to use my own keys."

I inched towards my bedroom window, trying to decide whether it would be worth the jump down. I would probably end up breaking my leg just like my mother had and we certainly didn't need two of us in wheelchairs, although if I stayed here I may end up dead. That was probably worse.

"I looked around the Christmas Shop for something to hurt Claire with and those solid, metal icicle ornaments were just sitting right there," Jill said. "So I grabbed one and stabbed her in the stomach with it. Can you believe Claire had the audacity to be upset when I told her I wasn't going to call her an ambulance? Like I would save her life after she had ruined mine. But I realized that I couldn't just take the rap for it. So I ran upstairs and got a cigar from that package I told you was for my dad. I mean, it was for my dad, but it also worked perfectly to plant evidence. I spread the ashes around so that it would look like Rich had been there. I figured between that and the keys, they would never suspect me."

Jill scoffed. We were quiet for a moment and I thought I could hear the noise of someone getting closer to my room. After you live somewhere for so long, you know all of the noises in the house. I decided to clue whoever it was into what was happening in my room.

"Can you just put the gun down Jill?" I said, a little more loudly than normal. I hoped whoever was lurking in the hallway was someone who had come to find me and not a lost party guest stumbling around looking for a bathroom.

Jill threw her head back and laughed. I had the feeling that if something didn't happen soon, she was going to use that gun on me. I was running out of time and the wine was making it hard to have any great ideas. The only idea it was giving me was to just risk it and jump out the window.

"I really won't tell anyone about the murder," I said, loudly again. "I just need you to put the gun down. You can leave right now and no one will ever

227

know except you and me."

"Yeah right," she scoffed. "Why in the world would I do that? I've learned I can't trust anyone except myself. The people I get close to just take advantage of me and throw me to the side. I'm not going to let that happen again."

As Jill continued to rant about the injustices of her life, I saw the door crack open behind her. I tried not to stare at the space so that I didn't alert Jill to it. I hoped whoever was on the other side was someone who could offer me some real help.

"Jill, I'm willing to listen, but I need you to put down the gun," I said, snapping my eyes towards the slightly open door, hoping that whoever was outside heard what I said and could come up with a good plan.

I realized that I needed to get her to move slightly towards me because if she stayed that close to the door, they wouldn't be able to open it far enough to do anything except enrage the woman with the gun by hitting her with the door.

"Jill, come on over here and sit down," I said, beckoning her towards me. She took one step closer to me and then stopped, suspicious of what I wanted.

"No, I'm the one that gives the orders right now," Jill said. She continued to talk about people she trusted letting her down, so I tried to tune her out and come up with another plan.

Straight up asking didn't get me far. What else could I do? I glanced slowly around my room until my eyes landed on the window next to my bed again. I couldn't actually jump out of it, but what if I just pretended to? That could give the person outside enough room to open the door and help.

I stood up and shuffled sideways towards the window, never taking my eyes off of the gun. I wanted to be ready in case I saw her start to pull the trigger.

"What are you doing?" Jill demanded. "Sit back down."

"I'm not just going to sit here and let you shoot me Jill," I said, continuing to inch over. "I'm going to open this window and jump out."

Jill squinted her eyes at me as if she were trying to figure out if I were serious or not. I got to the window and pulled it open. An icy blast shot inside, blowing snowflakes all over the room. The sheer, cream colored curtain panels on either side of the window blew around wildly between Jill and I.

I turned and looked at Jill. I didn't know how close I would have to get to actually climbing out of the window, but I was hoping I didn't have to actually start putting my leg out. I waited for her to make a move, but she still stood staring at me.

I sat my bottom on my windowsill, careful not to put too much of myself out of the window. The last thing I needed was to actually fall out of the window while pretending to jump out of the window. It worked because Jill started to stride towards me. She dropped the gun to her side in one hand while she reached out towards me with the other. I couldn't tell whether she was going to grab me or push me.

The door slammed open just as the curtains blew up again. I looked back at Jill who was within arm's reach and wondered if whoever had opened the door would make it to me in time.

•Chapter Thirty-Six•

The crash of the door opening into the desk was enough to startle Jill and stop her in her tracks. I jumped up from my perch on the windowsill and threw myself onto my bed as I watched Clark tackle Jill to the floor. Trina came flying in after him and snatched the gun off of the floor while my other sister Tilly dashed past everyone and slammed the window shut. Mandy came in and helped Clark subdue Jill.

I sat on my bed for a moment, frozen while my mind tried to wrap around what had just happened. Clark was sitting on Jill's back, trying to keep her pinned without actually hurting her. Trina was holding the gun delicately, trying hard not to destroy any evidence that may be on it.

"Are you okay?" Clark asked.

"Yeah, I'm okay," I said. "She didn't actually do anything to me."

"But I would have," Jill said in a low grunt. She started to cry, but her sobs were muffled by the floor.

"I'm going to go get Max," Tilly said before she dashed back out of the door. Now that the door was opened, I could hear the party still going on downstairs. The jazz band was playing a lively Christmas song and from the sounds of it, there were people dancing. I had almost completely forgotten about the party going on. When you stare down the barrel of a gun, a lot of things get erased out of your mind.

"How did you know to come help me?" I asked.

"Well we didn't at first," Clark said. "Trina had told me about your surprise for your mom. I figured you'd be back down in a few minutes after Jill came, but it had been a long time. So I asked Trina if she had seen you yet. When she said no, we went to find Mandy."

"I said I had no idea where you were," Mandy said from beside me. "So together we decided to come up and figure out what happened. Just as we got into the family area, we heard you saying something about a murder and a gun, so we knew that whatever was going on wasn't good."

"We crept up to the door," Trina said. "When we cracked it open, we could see the gun in Jill's hand. So we made our plan, but Jill was too close to the door."

"Yeah, how did you know to have her move closer to you?" Clark said.

"I may have had a few glasses of wine, but I could still tell that the door wouldn't be able to open much with where she was standing," I said. "So I knew that for anyone to safely get in here and help me, I would have to get her to come away from the door. I'm just glad I didn't fall out of that window."

Mandy was smiling at me and as we reached a lull in the conversation, she reached over and gave me a big squeeze. I collapsed into her arms and let her hold me up for a little while. After a minute, I sat back up and looked at Clark and Trina keeping Jill subdued.

"But let me tell you, I was relieved it was you guys and not some lost party guest looking for a bathroom instead," I said.

We all laughed, except Jill who was softy crying. I couldn't help but feel bad for her, so I got off of my bed and knelt down beside her.

"Jill," I said. She looked at me and I used a tissue I had grabbed to dry her eyes and cheeks. "I forgive you. You might not say that you are sorry, but I do forgive you. I understand how lousy your situation was."

I reached over and squeezed her hand. I was surprised to feel her squeeze back, just a little.

Max and Tilly came thundering down the hallway and ran into my bedroom. Max stumbled backward a step as he looked around and I didn't blame him. Trina and Clark were sitting on Jill, who was still clad in her giant, puffy purple winter coat. I was knelt down beside her while Mandy was on the bed. A gun was just sitting on the floor, out of anyone's reach. And there was snow quickly melting all over my room from when I had opened the window.

"What in the world?" Max said. "I'm not exactly sure what is going on, but I can see it isn't good."

I gave Max a quick summary of what had happened including the fact that Jill was Claire's killer. I could see a sort of relief pass over Max's face when I told him that Rich wasn't the killer. I felt the same way, but I would feel even better when the adrenaline stopped pumping through my veins.

"I've already called for someone to come and arrest her," he said. "And it looks like so far you've all got it covered. I will just secure the gun."

A few seconds later, the wail of squad cars got closer and closer. I ran out of the room and to the top of the large staircase. The street outside suddenly had four squad cars come screeching up, all with lights and sirens blaring. Eight officers came charging in the front door, weapons drawn, and looked around, obviously unaware of the party that was happening.

"Up here," I yelled. "The murderer is up here."

Several of the party guests who happened to be in the front room turned and looked at me with horror written across their faces. I realized that made it sound like someone had been killed at the party, so I knew I had to say something.

"No one died up here," I yelled. "This is a murderer from a previous murder."

That didn't make anything better. In fact, it seemed to almost make things worse. The ridiculousness of the situation made all of the wine I had drank earlier in the evening catch up to me. I started giggling and couldn't stop.

My mother suddenly rolled out of the living room in her wheelchair pushed by my father. Her face wore a mask of concern. Apparently a jazz band wasn't enough to make them miss the parade of officers who came in the door and my yelling about a murderer.

"Are you alright Tessa?" my mother asked. My father gave me a stern look, obviously thinking I had been drinking much more than I actually had been.

"I'm okay Mom and Dad," I said as I walked down the stairs. "I didn't mean to ruin the party. And I'm sorry to say, but your surprise isn't here Mom. Well, unless you count this spectacle."

As I gestured towards the stairs, the parade of officers was back. The first two were doing crowd control while two more were carrying Jill in handcuffs. Behind them were two more officers with evidence bag and the last two were walking with Max. As Max got to the bottom of the staircase, he walked over to my parents and I.

"I hate to break up your party Mr. and Mrs. Schmidt," Max said. "But your daughter apprehended a murderer just now upstairs and I'll need her to come down to the station and answer some questions."

My parents both slowly turned to look at me, their jaws hanging open. I shrugged my shoulders. I wasn't really sure what to say and I wasn't going to tell them the whole story in the middle of our party.

"Come on Tessa," Max said. "You can ride with me."

Max grabbed our jackets and helped me into mine. I promised my parents that I would fill them in on everything when I got back and that they should keep up the party fun. Max and I stepped out into the cold, December air and I looked around at the beauty of winter around us. We rode to the police station in silence, but Max did hold my hand as we drove under all of the lights that were on in downtown.

I looked out at the giant town Christmas tree and laughed a little bit.

"What's so funny?" Max asked with a puzzled look on his face. Most people threatened with a gun were probably not so merry.

"Here I was so worried about how the party would go," I said. "In all of the scenarios I went through in my head about things going wrong, in none of them did I consider that a murderer would threaten me with a gun."

•Chapter Thirty-Seven•

I was sitting in the more comfortable interview room at the police station sipping a cup of hot chocolate that one of the secretaries had brought in for me. I knew the other interview room was bare, with only a metal table and a few uncomfortable chairs to sit in. My interview room had cushy chairs and some pictures on the wall. There was even a fern plant sitting in one corner. This was the room they put people like me who had unwittingly caught a murderer.

When I got to the police station, I had been brought in here and two police officers who were not Max had taken my statement. They asked a few questions, but I had tried to be pretty thorough so soon enough, they had left the room, leaving me to sit and wait. The magazines they had left me were not that interesting. At least, they were not interesting enough to be of any use after the first ten minutes of my wait. I didn't care much for Fishing and Hunting Quarterly or Midwestern Gardens.

The next time the door opened, Max came him. He gave me a sly smile and I knew that the smile was the flirtiest thing I'd get. He was in work mode as Officer Marcus now. Thankfully Officer Marcus was a pretty genial sort of guy.

"Hey Tessa," he said. "So Jill confessed to everything: the murder and threatening you. She didn't try to hide anything. I think she knew that we had her."

I nodded my head. I was glad she hadn't made it anymore difficult. She had told me everything and I had no reason to lie. It was easier for her if she came clean.

"Jill told us that she and Claire had known each other and that Claire had ruined her life," Max said. "Somehow we had not realized that anyone in town actually knew Claire."

"I actually didn't know either, until Jill herself let it slip," I said.

"Jill said she thought you knew from the time you came to her apartment a few days ago," Max said. "She said that you saw a few things and she thought you invited her to the party to expose her as the murderer there."

I was taken a bit aback. I had a bizarre image in my head of me stopping the jazz band and making an announcement to all of the guests that we had a murderer in our midst before asking her to come up on stage with me. In my daydream mind, there was a stage and microphone in my living room.

"I still wasn't sure until tonight when she was acting so weird and finally pulled the gun out," I said. "I knew she had been acting strange, but I tried to just

238

tell myself that she had been so close to the murder and the murderer that it freaked her out. I guess that is still true, in a way."

Max nodded and for a moment we sat in silence. We were both still in our holiday party clothes. My mind went back to my parents and I hoped they would forgive me for causing a ruckus at their big party. I hadn't meant to, of course, but I had.

"I'm sorry that I had to take you away from your party," Max said. Sometimes it was like that boy could read my mind.

"That's alright," I said. "I just hope my parents aren't too worried about me."

"I'm sure your sisters will tell them everything," Max said. "You are free to go. But if you don't mind missing more of the party, maybe you and I could go have a drink together."

His voice dropped to a whisper when he said the last part. Obviously pretty much everyone in the police department knew about Max and I, but it still would look really bad if they caught an officer asking a witness out for a drink after their interview at the police station.

I grabbed my coat off of the back of my chair and together we walked out the door and into the snowy night. Max parked in the parking lot across from the Loony Bin and together we ran across the street. Before we went inside, Max stopped and turned to me.

"I do have an ulterior motive," Max said with a twinkle in his eye. "I'm also here to tell Rich's children that he will be let out and that they should go pick him up. Just don't tell them that he used his one call to call Sue, okay? Ready for some fun?"

My night could certainly use a happy pick-me-up, so I nodded at him. Max opened the door for me and held it so I could go in first. I let him take the lead once we were inside and followed him when he walked right up to the counter.

Just like the last time we were in there, Rich's children all scowled at us. Marie especially had a sour look on her face.

"Oh I know you are unhappy with me, but I come bearing good news," Max said. "All of you come over here."

Rich's kids all looked at each other in confusion as they moved down to the end of the bar in front of us. They all looked around like they weren't sure exactly what was about to happen.

"Tonight Tessa here caught Claire's real murderer so we are letting your dad go," Max said with a big smile on his face. All of Rich's kids burst into cheers and the entire bar whooped and howled at the good news. There was even a round of applause from the regulars.

"You guys get out of here and go pick him up,"

Max said. "He's going to need a ride home."

"But who will watch the bar?" Charlie asked.

"Tessa and I will," Max said. "But only if you promise not to be gone too long."

I laughed in delight as Max and I were each handed an apron that we slipped on over our party clothes. Charlie, Marie and their brother Brian ran out through the kitchen and Max as I took our places behind the counter.

Thankfully the bar was filled with regulars who took it easy on us. I couldn't help but laugh along the first time I tried to pour a beer from the tap ended up with a mug of foam instead. Max was being given a hard time for not knowing how to mix anything besides a whiskey sour or rum and coke. I found the chalk and changed the daily drink special on the chalkboard behind the bar to a whiskey sour, much to the enjoyment of the crowd.

Someone figured out how to turn up the volume on the speakers and put on some classic Christmas music. We all sang along and I felt like I was at the after party of my Christmas party. I spotted myself in the mirror and couldn't help but notice how happy I looked. My hair was flying all over having escaped out of the bun I had fashioned earlier. My cheeks were red from the wine, the warmth, and the laughter I was surrounded with.

The next time I went by Max, he pointed up.

When I looked, I saw that one of the regulars was standing on his stool and holding a piece of mistletoe above us. Max dipped me low and kissed me hard on the lips. That mistletoe was getting me into some hot spots tonight.

When it got to the point where I finally felt like I didn't ever actually want to be a bartender, the front door opened and I turned to see Rich walking in. The crowd in the bar erupted once more and everyone surged forward, trying to be the first to welcome Rich to his domain.

Rich fought his way to the bar, holding Sue's hand. His children came behind him. When he got behind the bar with us, he climbed up on top and motioned for the crowd to be quiet. Once they had brought the noise down, he gave a little speech.

"I'm so happy to be back here with you all. It isn't often you see a cop behind the bar here."

Max roared with laughter and the crowd chuckled along before Rich kept going with his speech.

"While I was in jail, I had some time to think. See, I was married for so long that I never really thought about ever falling in love again. But then I met Sue and she was thinking the same thing. Somehow, we accidentally fell in love. But I didn't want my kids to think I was forgetting about their mom. So Sue and I kept our love to ourselves."

"No you didn't, we all knew," came a yell from the crowd. Everyone laughed because it had been one of those open sorts of secrets in Shady Lake.

"Okay, we weren't that secret about it. But I tried my hardest to not rub it in my kid's face. When I was brought in for questioning, I made Sue swear not to tell anyone that the night of the murder we were together. But after everything went down and I was sitting by myself in a jail cell, I promised myself that when I got out I would never hide our love again."

Sue was looking at him with shining eyes. She looked so genuinely happy and in love that it made her look like she was closer to being a teenager than to the retirement age she really was. I was glad to see the spark was back inside of her.

"Sue come on up here," Rich said.

Sue shook her head, but Max came over and helped boost her up to stand next to Rich on the bar.

"I want to spend the rest of my life with you, no matter how short that time may be for us old geezers," Rich said before getting down on one knee. "I don't have a ring for you, but I will buy you whatever you want if you agree to marry me."

Sue clapped her hands over her mouth in shock and nodded yes. I glanced over at Rich's kids to see their reactions and I was pleasantly surprised to see them all smiling. Marie was even crying a little bit. Maybe all of Rich's worrying had been for nothing

243

or maybe having their father in jail had changed their minds about Sue.

As Sue and Rich shared a kiss on the bar of the Loony Bin, I realized that it was close to midnight and I should probably get back to see how the party was going or not going at this point. Max nodded at me and we went quietly through the front door, leaving the celebration behind for a walk in the silent snow to the car.

•Chapter Thirty-Eight•

The jazz band was playing their last set when Max and I walked in the front door. We weren't even able to get our jackets off before being bombarded by party guests who were wondering what had happened.

"Can I tell them the story?" I asked Max.

"You can tell your family, but the rest will have to wait and read it in the Shady Lake Tribune tomorrow," Max winked. Chelsea scoffed behind him, counting that as a victory. I decided to give her this one and told her to stick around after the party for the full story.

I nodded and Max swept me into his arms, twirling around the entry hall to the jazzy number the band was playing. The wine had mostly worn off by now, but I was still feeling like my head was swimming. I almost couldn't believe everything that had happened today. I would be glad when it was time to get in bed but for now, I was in the arms of a handsome man and the party I had put together was still a raging success.

The guests cleared out, mostly with the help of Ronald who told everyone that now that the band was done, anyone left would be privy to listening to him practice his campaign speeches for next year.

That cleared the room pretty quickly.

My parents, siblings, Max, Clark, and Chelsea quickly cleared away the dishes and put food away. We cleaned up as much as we could and then headed upstairs to the living room so that I could tell them everything that had happened and everything I knew about the murder.

Max decided he should leave as he had already heard everything and he was needed back at work early tomorrow morning which by this point, was in just a few hours. I let him hold me tight by the front window as we watched the snow continue to fall. After a good night kiss, I waved to him through the window as he backed his car out of the driveway.

I walked upstairs to a captive audience. My parents were on the couch along with Trina. Tilly and Teddy were in the arm chairs while Tank, Clark, and Chelsea had been relegated to the floor. I assumed my nieces and nephew were sleeping somewhere, so I was able to tell the entire story, start to finish without censoring anything.

Once I finished, Chelsea got up to hurry out and get the story in the paper the next day. I knew she wanted to get a jump on all of the out of town journalists, so Clark and I walked her to the front door. For once, I felt like we actually were getting along.

"I was supposed to give you one warning," I

said to her before she left. "Don't give all of the gritty details. Just do more of the story."

"I will," Chelsea said, rolling her eyes. "It'll be my Christmas gift to you."

She slammed the door behind her and I tried not to laugh as she slipped her way on the ice down to her car. She didn't actually fall, so I felt like it was okay that I laughed because it serves her right. Clark gave me a disapproving look which made me laugh even harder.

I slipped on my jacket to walk Clark out to the porch once Chelsea was out of sight. Hand in hand, we paused once we were out the door. It was snowing and the wind was blowing just enough to make it look like a snow globe outside. I realized that for the first time since Thanksgiving, I felt like I could actually breath and enjoy the holiday season. I reveled in the bright lights from the house that were lighting up the cold winter night.

"I actually have something to give you," Clark said, letting go of my hand.

Clark dug his hand into his pocket and pulled something out but before he showed it to me, he paused for a moment and all of the color drained from his face. For just a moment, I wondered if he had an engagement ring and he was going to propose to me. I tried to stop my eyes from getting wide. Clark was a great guy, but I did not want to get married to anyone right now.

"Is something wrong?" I asked. My voice shook a little bit, but Clark didn't seem to notice.

"No, not wrong," Clark said. "But I just realized that this is something you may not actually want to keep."

I gave him a puzzled look and waited while he seemed to decide what to do about it. He had told me about it, so now he had to give it to me, right?

"You can't just leave it at that and not show me what it is," I said. "That is totally unfair."

"Okay, but promise you won't be weird about it?" Clark said.

I thought about that for a second. If it was an engagement ring, I couldn't promise I wouldn't be weird about it. My mind was racing a bit, trying to figure out what the gift was.

"I promise I won't be weird," I said. What else was I supposed to say?

Clark stepped back and opened his hand in front of him. In his hand was one of the Christmas necklaces I had admired in the Christmas Shop. The silver chain had alternating baubles made from red and green wire. It was one that had been lovingly handmade by Jill. I start to laugh and it wasn't a cutesy "I love my gift" laugh. It was a low, unattractive gut laugh.

I bent over in half and held my stomach as I

laughed so hard I couldn't catch my breath. I couldn't help myself. What were the odds that the present I was getting was made by someone who had literally tried to kill me just hours before?

Clark looked horrified for a moment and I felt bad because it wasn't his fault. He had absolutely no way of knowing how the evening was going to go before he had a chance to give me my gift.

Finally, I was able to stop laughing and catch my breath. I took a few deep breaths to try to calm myself down a little bit before I said anything.

"It is beautiful Clark," I said between giggles. "I really do love it. It will always remind me of you and of this night."

"That's kind of what I'm afraid of," Clark said quietly.

"I didn't mean it like that," I said. "Well, I kind of meant it like that, but not in a hurtful way. Just that this night was very memorable."

Clark gave a shy smile. He was usually pretty personable and outgoing, so it was unusual to see him so put out. I hurriedly gave him a big hug around the middle. When I tilted my head back, he leaned down and gave me a kiss that was a bit less passionate than the one earlier in the night, but romantic nonetheless.

After holding each other for a bit longer, Clark helped me put on the necklace before he climbed carefully down the icy front steps and into his pickup truck. I waved him out of sight and headed back inside, happy for this day to finally be over.

As I got ready for bed that night, I knew that the rest of the holiday season would only get better from here on out. It had to because I don't think I'd be facing down a gun hanging partway out a window into the cold again. After that, I know I can handle managing the rest of family Christmas. I drifted off to sleep and dreamed that night of a Christmas party. At this Christmas party though, I was able to enjoy the music and company rather than face down death.

•About the Author•

Linnea West lives in Minnesota with her husband and two children. She taught herself to read at the age of four and published her first poem in a local newspaper at the age of seven. After a turn as a writer for her high school newspaper, she went to school for English Education and Elementary Education. She didn't start writing fiction until she was a full time working mother. Besides reading and writing, she spends her time chasing after her children, watching movies with her husband, and doing puzzle books. Learn more about her and her upcoming books by visiting her website and signing up for her newsletter at linneawestbooks.com.

Note From the Author: Reviews are gold to authors! If you've enjoyed this book, would you consider rating it and reviewing it on Amazon? Thank you!

•Other Books in the Series•

Small Town Minnesota Cozy Mystery Series
Book One-Halloween Hayride Murder
Book Two-Christmas Shop Murder
Book Three-Winter Festival Murder
Book Four-Valentine's Blizzard Murder
Book Five-Spring Break Murder

Made in the USA
Coppell, TX
10 November 2019